I really wanted to see him again but...

"We'll probably get back late," Lacey went on. "All I need is for you to handle a call from my dad. If he phones your house, tell him the team went out to eat together and everybody's doing homework at your house."

I thought about it for a moment. "What if he wants to speak to you?"

"He won't," she replied. She sounded absolutely sure. "I'm counting on you to be cool about this—Jessy with the messy golden hair," she added. "So how do you like Rocky?"

"He's cute," I said. And my only excuse to see him was Lacey.

"You know, if you had gotten me that team shirt, tomorrow's escape would have been a lot easier to pull off," Lacey said.

I just followed her through the park gates silently. Nothing had been easy since the day I'd started at the junior high. And I was pretty sure tomorrow wasn't going to be any different.

SWEET VALLEY jr. high

Soulmates

Written by
Jamie Suzanne

Created by
FRANCINE PASCAL

BANTAM BOOKS
NEW YORK • TORONTO • LONDON • SYDNEY • AUCKLAND

To Susan and Anders Johansson

RL 4, 008-012

SOULMATES

A Bantam Book / April 1999

Sweet Valley Junior High is a trademark of
Francine Pascal.

Conceived by Francine Pascal.

 Produced by 17th Street Productions,
a division of Daniel Weiss Associates, Inc.
33 West 17th Street, New York, NY 10011.

ISBN: 0-553-48605-5

Published simultaneously in the United States and Canada

Bantam Books are published by Bantam Books, a division of Random
House, Inc. Its trademark, consisting of the words "Bantam Books" and
the portrayal of a rooster, is Registered in the U.S. Patent and Trademark
Office and in other countries. Marca Registrada. Bantam Books, 1540
Broadway, New York, New York 10036.

PRINTED IN THE UNITED STATES OF AMERICA

OPM   0 9 8 7 6 5 4 3 2 1

Jessica

Why did I come here? I wondered as I wandered around the Red Bird Mall. *It isn't cheering me up.*

I had come to the mall to participate in my favorite hobby—shopping. Usually nothing makes me happier. But not this time. First of all, I had no money. Second of all, I was by myself.

How loserish can you get?

As I walked the circle around the edge of the food court, I noticed a group of boys standing in front of Chip's Chocolate Chips, munching cookies. Two of the four guys were pretty cute. If I weren't by myself, I would have smiled at them.

But right now, I was just grateful those guys didn't know who I was. That's why I came to the Red Bird Mall instead of going to the Valley Mall, which is closer to my house. If I ran into anybody from my old school while I was pathetically window shopping by myself, I would positively die. The fact is, last year I used to rule

1

the school. Sweet Valley Middle School was my domain, and I was, like, the queen of everything I looked at or whatever.

Anyway, so now I was at a new school, where I was *not* the queen. My twin, Elizabeth, and I transferred to Sweet Valley Junior High at the beginning of the year, and I am not exaggerating when I say that my new school is worse than a torture chamber filled with blood-sucking trolls.

I love it there, as you can tell.

I stared at my reflection in the shiny food court sign. Was I different this year or something? Was that why I wasn't popular? I didn't *look* any different. But maybe other people could see things I couldn't.

"What are you looking at?" I growled at myself, then spun around—and came face-to-face with Lacey Frells. I had to stop myself from groaning.

Lacey was the coolest girl at Sweet Valley Junior High—the coolest girl in the *world,* maybe. And she didn't like me. About a week ago I told her this little white lie that she totally blew out of proportion, and then she decided I was a dork. I won't go into what the lie was. That's a whole other story.

The important thing is that I never managed to impress her and thus never managed to make it into the cool crowd at SVJH. And thus I was now shopping alone and talking to myself like a lame loser freak.

"Hello, Jessica," Lacey said levelly, running one hand through her sleek sun-streaked brown hair. Her other hand stretched back behind her, anchored by a little girl with blond curls.

"Hi." I tried to smile. Why was she talking to me? I never thought she'd want to speak to me again after last week. "What are you doing here?" It was an idiotic question, but I couldn't think of anything better.

Lacey shrugged. "I'm baby-sitting my half sister, Penelope." She flicked her head back in the direction of the girl, who looked about three years old. "Lucky me."

Penelope's round blue eyes were swollen with tears, and her bottom lip stuck out in a pout. She clung to a white stuffed rabbit.

"Hi, Penelope," I said. "I'm Jessica." I pointed to the stuffed animal. "What's your rabbit's name?" I asked.

"Bunny."

"Bunny." I grinned. "Well, that's easy to remember."

Penelope smiled back at me. She seemed sweet.

I looked back at Lacey. So, was I, like, supposed to make conversation with her? I racked my brain to come up with something to say, but luckily I didn't have to.

"Hey—Lacey!" someone called. Lacey stiffened.

3

I followed her gaze and saw two supercool girls walking toward us. They looked about three years older than us. I wondered who they were.

Lacey cast a nervous glance at Penelope, then seemed to recover. As the girls approached, Lacey casually dropped her sister's hand, then closed and opened her eyes slowly, her dark lashes sweeping down over her cheeks. I'd never met anyone who could blink as cool as her.

"Hi, Cameron," she said to one of the girls— the taller one with short, spiky black hair. "Hey, Dakota."

Dakota's head was covered in tiny dreads, and she wore wire-rimmed glasses. "Who's this?" she asked, eyeing me.

"This is Jessica," Lacey said finally, "a girl from school."

A girl from school? Well, at least she didn't say, "This is Jessica, the biggest loser I've ever met," I decided. Would Lacey ever say something like, *"This is Jessica, my friend"?* If only. Being friends with Lacey would solve a lot of my problems. "Hi," I said to Cameron and Dakota.

Out of the corner of my eye I noticed that the four cute guys I had spotted before were staring at our group of girls. I wasn't surprised. Lacey and her two friends were totally gorgeous and way, way, cool. I slouched a little bit, trying to look like I belonged with this group.

One of the guys—I didn't see which—tossed a small foil ball over our heads, which landed just in front of our feet.

Penelope picked up the ball.

"Brat!" Lacey muttered to Penelope between her teeth.

Cameron grinned, and Dakota gave a little chuckle.

"It's no big deal," I said quietly to Lacey. I knew Penelope didn't mean to be a problem. As for the guys, they were just trying to get us to notice them.

Penelope tossed the ball back to the boys. They laughed, then threw two more balls of foil, which landed in front of us.

"I'm glad I'm past that stage," Dakota said.

"It's so *junior high*," Lacey agreed.

Well, you and I are in *junior high,* I thought, but I didn't say anything. Then one of the guys—a dark-haired boy in huge athletic shoes—sprinted ahead, swooped by us, and snatched Penelope's stuffed rabbit.

Penelope let out an incredible howl. Everyone in the food court turned around. The howl became heavy sobs.

"Give it back," I said without even thinking. "Give back her rabbit."

Cameron and Dakota looked at each other.

"Later, Lacey," Cameron said, and the two of them walked away quickly.

"Later," Lacey replied. She sounded *furious*. I guess she didn't want to look like a nerd in front of her cool friends any more than I wanted to look like a nerd in front of *her*.

The four guys grinned at one another. I couldn't believe they weren't giving back the rabbit—couldn't they see how upset Penelope was? Well, fine. I would just *take* it back. But as I reached for Bunny, the dark-haired boy who had grabbed the toy quickly tossed it to the boy wearing the Giants shirt. Lacey took Penelope's hand, walked over to a table, and sat down. Lacey was shaking her head and saying something under her breath. *Why isn't she standing up to them?* I wondered.

"Do you think stealing a little kid's rabbit is cool or something?" I asked the dark-haired guy.

In response, the blond boy held the toy out to me. My fingers were just closing around it when he snatched it away and took off. Penelope shrieked.

"Don't worry, I'll get it back," I called to Penelope. I ran after the guy.

He raced through the crowd, dodging left and right. So did I. People stepped out of his way, then out of mine. "Go get him, girl," some old lady yelled.

The boy took a sharp turn at the fountain. Closer still. I could hear his friends running after us.

This is so lame, I thought. *I can't believe I'm doing this. Lacey's never going to speak to me again.* At least Cameron and Dakota weren't around to see me chasing after Bunny—I would have been mortified. But I don't give up on something once I've started it. I hate to lose.

At the far side of the fountain I reached out—in one second that boy was dead meat. "Heads up!" he hollered, and tried to toss Bunny over the water to his friends. He missed.

Splash!

Bunny belly-flopped into the fountain. The four guys and I stared at it for a moment, floating facedown among the plastic lily pads. Then they all cracked up. Some other people standing around the fountain laughed with them. I was so mad that I couldn't even move. I saw a long arm reach in and fish Bunny out of the water.

I stared at the soggy rabbit, which was now Ty-D-Bol blue. Gross.

"Finders keepers, Damon," the dark-haired boy joked. "It's yours now."

I looked up—right into the eyes of Damon Ross.

My stomach flipped over.

Damon was possibly the cutest guy at school and my personal hero. He had recently rescued me from two jerks who were teasing me at my locker.

"I think you're going to have to get another rabbit," he said.

I could feel strands of my hair sticking to my face. My cheeks were hot and probably red. "It's not mine."

"Oh," was all he said as he wrung out the toy. I guessed he'd been sitting on the edge of the fountain, eating, because he picked up a napkin from beneath a plate of hamburger and gently blotted the rabbit.

Damon sure had a way of showing up in the middle of my uncoolest moments. The day he rescued me at my locker, he had thought he was standing up for Elizabeth. Did he think he was helping out my twin again?

He held the rabbit by its ears and handed it to me, smiling a little.

"Thanks. And just so you know, I'm Jessica," I said, "not Elizabeth."

"I figured," he replied, then sat down to finish his burger.

What did that *mean?* I wondered as I headed back to the food court to find Lacey.

For a moment I was afraid she had cleared out of there, not wanting to be seen with the kind of loser who would chase a rabbit through the mall. But I found her sitting at the table, Penelope across from her. The little girl held up her arms when she saw me with the rabbit. Her eyes got wider. "He's *blue!*"

"It's the newest shade for fall," I told her, sitting down.

Lacey smirked.

"Careful, Bunny is a little drippy," I added, handing the toy to Penelope. "He's been for a swim."

"I just saw those guys go by," Lacey said, her smirk becoming more of a smile. "The blond one looked wiped out. But you don't look tired at all."

"Spare me—I look awful," I replied, opening my purse to get out a mirror. "In case you're interested, Damon Ross rescued Bunny from the fountain."

"Damon? He's cool," Lacey said, "for a ninth-grader." I hoped he was cool enough to make up for the fact that I had just made an idiot out of myself. Lacey did that blinking thing again. "Do you like to run, Jessica?"

"Run?" Was this a trick question? "Uh, it's all right, I guess. I ran with my brother early this summer when things got boring."

"So why don't you join the cross-country team?" she suggested.

Join the *track* team? Did she have, like, a brain transplant while I was chasing the rabbit? Or was she making fun of me?

9

"*I'm* going to," she added.

"You are?" I blurted out. "At Sweet Valley Middle, that kind of sport is nerdy." As soon as I'd said it, I wished I hadn't. I had to learn to keep my mouth shut till I found out what was in at my new school.

Lacey gazed at me steadily. "I don't let anybody tell me what I should or shouldn't do."

That's what made Lacey so cool and even a little scary. She really didn't care what anybody else thought of her. I used to be more like that, but as much as I hated to admit it, I *did* care what Lacey thought of me. Was she starting to think I was less of a nerd? I could hardly believe we were sitting there, having a somewhat normal conversation.

I tapped my fingers on the table, thinking. *Should* I run track? Joining the team would give me a chance to know Lacey better. And then maybe I could hang with her cool friends instead of by myself at the mall. Joining the cross-country team would mean not trying out for the cheer squad—but maybe cheerleading wasn't cool at SVJH. I remembered Lacey saying something about cheerleading being lame one time. *Forget it, then,* I decided.

"Miss Scarlett tried to coach a girls' team last year," Lacey went on, "but everyone hates her, so not enough kids joined."

"Yeah?"

"Mrs. Krebs, the bio teacher, offered to do it this year. She's nice. She'll probably let anybody—like the off-season guy jocks—run with us."

This was sounding better and better.

"It would be cool if you went out for the team with me," Lacey added. She studied her nails. "Those girls I was talking to before—Cameron and Dakota," she said, seemingly out of the blue, "you know who they are?"

I shook my head.

"They used to be in Splendora."

My jaw dropped to the floor. "They did? Really?" I asked. Splendora was the most popular local band in Sweet Valley. Lots of kids said they were going to go national one day. "How do you know them?" I asked.

"I hang out with Splendora sometimes." She shrugged as if it were no big deal.

"Wow," I said, because it *was* a big deal. An enormous deal. Lacey was even cooler than I had ever realized.

"Wow," Penelope echoed, like she knew what we were talking about. I laughed. Lacey ignored her.

"Those two have broken off to form their own band," she added. "I think they're going to be sorry, but who knows?"

I was hoping Lacey would tell me more, like

what the band members were like for real, but she didn't. She looked at me sideways. "Maybe you could meet the band sometime," she said. She shrugged again. "If you're interested. They rehearse every day around four. We could watch them after track practice one day."

"I'd love to," I said. I was trying not to sound too eager, but I couldn't really help it. How could Lacey act so cool all the time without even trying?

I'm going to meet Splendora—with Lacey! All I had to do was join cross-country. I was still amazed that Lacey was interested in the sport. I knew Lacey had a boyfriend in high school. Why didn't she want to spend time with him? *Maybe she and Gel broke up,* I thought, *and she's looking for something to do.* Well, once Lacey and I got to know each other better, she'd tell me things like that.

"So," I said, "when's sign-up?"

Lacey

"Guess who I ran into today?" I asked Kristin late Sunday afternoon.

"Vanilla Ice," she replied.

"No," I said patiently, wrapping the phone cord around my finger. I wished Kristin wouldn't try to be cute. She's my best friend, but that doesn't mean she never gets on my nerves. I adjusted the pillows behind my head and settled in more comfortably on top of my bed. "I ran into your pal, Jessica Wakefield."

"She isn't my *pal*," Kristin replied. "I hardly know her! I just think she's nice, that's all."

I rolled my eyes. "Nice doesn't pay, Kristin."

"Well, *I'm* nice."

"That's okay—I still like you," I assured her. "So guess what? She and I are going to join the track team together." I felt like laughing at that. How hilarious.

There was silence on the other end of the line. I frowned at the receiver. "Kristin? Hello?"

13

"The *track* team?" she asked. "Is this some kind of joke that I'm not sophisticated enough to get?"

I did laugh then.

"No. No joke. It's a *plan*. A brilliant idea I got today when Jessica went for a jog in the mall. Lamefield and I join the track team. I get a team shirt. Then I go hang with Gel or whoever after school, and nobody asks questions because they assume I'm at practice." I smiled, thinking about my father's state of blissful ignorance. Not that he would really care where I went after school anyway. "And when the team gets out of school early for meets, I pretend to take off with them and Jessie-Wessie covers for me."

"She'll never do it," Kristin said. She thinks she knows everything sometimes.

"Yes, she *will*," I insisted. "Once she heard I was going out for the team, she had to do it too. I told her that I knew Splendora, and she practi-cally bowed down to worship me."

"I don't think this is a very—," Kristin started.

At that moment my idiot half sister poked her head into my room. She had that disgusting blue rabbit with her. Needless to say, I didn't want that thing anywhere near me.

"Lacey?" she asked. "Will you play with me?"

"No! Get out of here!" I practically screamed. "Don't you know you're supposed to *knock?*"

Penelope closed the door and started crying.
Terrific. Now Penelope would run down the hall
and tell my stepmother that I was being mean
again, and—of course—my stepmother wouldn't
even bother to listen to *my* side of the story,
wouldn't even care that I was on the *phone*. . . .
That kid is the most obnoxious thing on the
planet. I swear, I can't *stand* her.

"Kristin? I have to go," I said quickly. "See you
in school, okay?"

"Bye, Lacey," she said.

I hung up the phone just in time to hear my
stepmother's patented three supershort knocks.

"Come in," I said sweetly. "Hi!" I said with a
bright smile as she stepped into my room. She
frowned. I knew what was coming—yell, yell,
yell, be nice to your sister, blah, blah. Who cared?

I couldn't wait to join the track team. It was
my ticket out of here.

Elizabeth

"Got any scissors, Lizzie?" my twin asked Sunday night.

"Depends on what you want to do with them," I teased.

"Style your hair," Jessica replied with a straight face, then stretched and reached out for the pair.

I rolled my eyes and handed them over. New school year, new school, new friends—everything was different for Jessica and me. But one thing had stayed the same: My twin putting off her homework till the last possible minute.

She lay sprawled on my bed, reading a magazine. It was a running magazine, though, not her usual beauty/gossip/fashion reading, which seemed a little strange for her. I was working at my desk on an old computer that had been passed down to us. Jessica had said I could keep the PC in my room as long as I didn't mind typing her projects for her. And I didn't. I loved having the computer for my own writing.

"What are you working on?" Jessica asked as she started to cut the magazine page in front of her.

"An article for the *Spectator.*"

The first week of class I had wanted more than anything to make the school newspaper—the *Spectator* has won awards as best in the county. But being on the paper isn't as great as I thought it would be. The girl who's the editor in chief, Charlie, thinks she's working at *The Wall Street Journal* and is heavily into barking orders and making the articles as boring as possible. My friends Salvador and Anna—they're on the paper too—spend most of their time at meetings rolling their eyes at each other.

If Salvador weren't there to crack me up, I don't know how I would stand the *Spec* meetings at all.

"Everything the *Spectator* publishes is so serious," I told Jessica. "I thought I'd try a funny piece."

"They could sure use a sense of humor," Jessica agreed.

"Something about school-bus etiquette," I continued. "Salvador suggested a parody of Miss Manners."

"A what?"

"An imitation that's supposed to be a joke," I explained.

"Riding the school bus is a joke," Jessica replied. Back at Sweet Valley Middle, we rode our bikes to school. My twin and I hated the bus.

"So give me some ideas," I said. "Some dos and don'ts for the polite bus rider."

"Don't lean close to the seat in front of you and keep burping up your breakfast."

"Like the guy we pick up at the corner of Elm and Windsor?"

"No matter where we sit, he always sits behind us," Jessica complained, flipping pages of the magazine. She cut out a second picture. "Don't eat cold pizza and pick at the cheeselike scabs."

"Gross!" I said. "Who does that?"

"The kid who gets on at Pinewood."

"Do bring a Ziploc bag if you plan to throw up," our brother, Steven, added as he passed by in the hall. "Hey," he said, backing up for a second glance through the door. "Jessica, is that my running magazine?"

"I guess," she said. "Maybe both of these are."

Steven stepped into the room. "You're cutting them up!" he exclaimed. "I haven't even read them yet!"

I glanced over my shoulder and saw two photos of girls in shiny running shorts and tops snipped from one of his magazines.

"Who's cutting up?" my father asked, coming in behind Steven. Dad likes to tease us out of getting into a full-blown fight over nothing. He dropped a pile of clean laundry on my bed. "Are you telling jokes? I heard one. Knock, knock—"

"No one's there," the three of us said quickly, trying to avoid another of Dad's terrible puns.

"Dad, Jessica took these out of my room," Steven complained, holding up the magazines and waving them around as if they were criminal evidence. *Maybe one day Steven will be a lawyer like Dad,* I thought. *He's so dramatic.*

"She went into my room and took them without my permission and now she's ripping them up." He opened one to a page with a big hole in the middle. "How am I supposed to read this?"

"You can't *read* it, Steven—it's a *picture,*" Jessica told him. "Duh."

"Jessica, you're going to have to tape those pages back together," Dad said. "And if Steven can't read the words, you'll need to replace the magazine."

"Got any tape, Lizzie?" Jessica asked, rolling off the bed. I tossed her the tape.

Dad handed Steven a pile of clean T-shirts and headed for the door.

"Hey, these aren't mine," Steven called after him just as Mom entered the room.

"Well, they came home in your gym bag," she said. "Need any help with your homework, girls?" She looked straight at Jessica.

Jessica sighed, then carried the magazine and

tape through the bathroom we share into her own room. Steven followed Dad down the hall.

"How's it going, Mom?" I asked when the others were gone. She was lugging around two big wallpaper books, doing her own homework—Mom's an interior decorator.

"Slowly," Mom replied. "Very slowly. My newest client can't stand any of the patterns I've selected for her. I've given her my best suggestions, and she thinks they're awful."

"Sounds like Charlie, my newspaper editor," I said.

"The one you and Salvador were talking about on the phone?" Mom asked.

I blinked. "How did you know it was Salvador?"

"I answered the phone, honey, remember?"

"Oh yeah, right."

"Besides," Mom added, "you talk to him in a different way than you talk to Anna."

"I do?" My heart was thudding in my chest. "I mean, no, I don't."

She just smiled. "Well, I think I'll go pick out the ugliest wallpaper I can find. My client will probably love it."

As soon as Mom left, I put my hands up to my cheeks, hoping they weren't warm. I didn't want to be blushing. Did I really talk differently to Salvador than to Anna? I hoped not. They were both my friends—I wanted to treat them the same.

And I wanted the fluttery feeling I got in my stomach whenever I thought about Salvador to go away.

I pushed that thought off the radar, glad I had something to keep my mind busy, like my school-bus article.

Some of the kids on our route were pretty rude. Hopefully they would laugh at my article, but then, later on, maybe some of them would think about how they acted. Salvador had said that's the way satire is supposed to work. He had been right about one thing: It was fun to write in a voice really different from my own. It was like becoming another person. I spent the next hour adding ideas and polishing my article. *I hope Salvador thinks it's funny,* I thought as I printed it out. *Maybe he'll want to draw a cartoon to go with my article. Then we could work together. . . .*

Oh. And maybe Anna will like it too.

Some Thoughts on Manners

Dear Reader,

It has recently come to Miss Perfect's attention that not everyone is as well behaved as she when riding the school bus. Perhaps a few dos and don'ts will help guide the rider to and from school as well as on class trips. Let's begin at the beginning.

When entering the school vehicle, do not announce in a loud voice, "This bus stinks." We all have a nose, and those who board the bus first get tired of hearing it over and over. Before riders get on the bus, I suggest that they remove their skates. If you choose to wear them, please do not suddenly grab the driver by the arm to keep yourself from rolling down the aisle. This may have some unhappy consequences when the driver is steering.

When moving down the aisle, it is best if those students carrying large band instruments and hockey sticks under their arms avoid sharp turns. If you happen to forget this advice, please say "excuse me" to the kid you whacked as soon as he is conscious again.

If there are no seats left on the bus except for the one next to you, please move your makeup mirror, mousse, comb, nail file, granola bars, juice box, and homework onto your own lap so another student can sit down. When doing last-minute homework, do not ask everyone else on the bus to look up words in their dictionaries and add up numbers on their calculators—especially those who are sleeping.

When falling asleep, the most polite thing to do is keep your head on your own shoulder. If you like to sing, avoid songs whose verses repeat and repeat and repeat. . . . Those putting on perfume, please aim carefully. Those carrying gym bags, please do not open them on the way home if you've had gym that day. That is why the bus stinks.

In conclusion, let us all try to have good manners and make every ride to and from school as perfect as I am.

Miss Perfect

Bethel

"Hey, Mary," I called happily. "Hey, Bonnie."

"Hey, Bethel," they called back as I jogged across the grass between the track and school. It was a breezy September afternoon, all gold and green, a great day for running.

I waved to them, then took a seat near the end of the splintery bench.

I couldn't believe how many girls were interested in cross-country running. Twenty-five, maybe more, all here after school on a Monday. It was probably because Mrs. Krebs was coaching the team—everybody liked her.

She was working her way slowly down the long bench at the edge of the school track. As she took down names and home phone numbers, I threaded laces through a new pair of training flats. I had lost my old ones at the end of last year. Big surprise—I also lost three library books and my report card on the same day. But running in these new ones would be like running on air. I'd feel twice as fast. The shoes were electric blue and, matched to a new pair of blue shorts, looked really sharp against my black skin.

I was leaning over, double knotting my laces, when I heard a girl nearby correct the coach in an annoyed voice, "It's *Lacey*. Lacey Frells."

I straightened up. Was my hearing all right? I looked in the direction of the voice, and sure enough, Queen Lacey gave me a long, cool stare. *She's just what our team needs,* I thought, *an unreliable snob.*

"Phone number, please?" Mrs. Krebs asked Lacey in her crisp British accent.

"You want my beeper number?" Lacey asked back.

"Your home phone will suffice," Krebsy replied with a smile.

"I didn't know you had a beeper," said the girl next to Lacey, sounding impressed. She was one of the new kids—one of the twins, who looked like she might want to grow up to be Barbie. I know you're not supposed to judge people by their looks, but sometimes I can't help it. This girl's bouncy blond hair just screamed "cheerleader." What were these two doing on the track team? Had I landed in some kind of alternate universe?

"Jessica Wakefield," the new kid said when Mrs. Krebs asked for her name. "I have a question."

"Yes?"

"I noticed that it's all girls today."

How observant, I thought.

"So what's your question, luv?" Mrs. Krebs asked.

"Aren't some of the off-season jocks, you know, the guys, going to run with us?"

I saw Lacey glance sideways at Jessica.

"No," Mrs. Krebs replied, shaking her head and looking puzzled. "No."

Well, those two are bye-bye, I thought. I wondered what had made them think we'd be running with guys.

"Hello, Bethel," Mrs. Krebs greeted me. "Phone number?"

I gave it to her and she moved on. Out of the corner of my eye I saw Lacey wiggling her finger, catching Jessica's attention, then pointing to my shoes. If they had known anything about running, they would have wished they were wearing my trainers. But Lacey's little upturned mouth told me she wouldn't be caught dead in a pair like mine.

"Like my shoes?" I asked Jessica, holding out my legs so she could see them clearly, curious how she'd respond.

She glanced at Lacey for a moment. "I prefer

mine," she said at last. "Of course, they're awfully expensive." She pointed her foot toward me.

"Great shoes," Jan Meier—who was sitting between us—said to Jessica. I rolled my eyes. *Why is Jan always so nice to everybody?*

"Yeah, they're perfect," I put in, "for your mother's aerobics class."

Jessica's eyes widened.

Before either of us could say any more, Mrs. Krebs asked for everyone's attention and began talking to the club about the importance of attending practice, supporting one another, doing our personal best, et cetera, et cetera. I'd been doing my personal best for the last three years. I kept my own running logs, always trying to beat my best time. My sister was a star runner—she got a full scholarship to Brown for track—and was the toughest coach I ever could have dreamed of. So I listened to Krebsy talk, but I also used the opportunity to check out the others.

Jan, who's no string bean, looked at our coach in disbelief as she laid out how she hoped to get us into long-distance running shape. Ginger Walters, a redhead whose long legs and long neck and splash of freckles always make me think of a giraffe, nervously bit her lip but looked interested. Mary Stillwater watched with serious dark eyes. Lacey looked totally bored.

One of these things is not like the other one, a voice sang in my head.

After the talk we crossed the track and spread out on the field encircled by it. Krebsy led us through warm-up stretches. Unfortunately I was stuck in the back of the group between Jessica and Lacey.

"Bend over and hang from the waist," Krebsy instructed.

Lacey gave a snort and pointed to Jan, who was having trouble reaching her toes. Jessica giggled. *That's nice,* I thought, *after Jan defended your shoes.* I glared at Jessica, but she didn't notice.

After a few more exercises the twenty-five of us were sprung. Just for four hundred meters, but I took flight, my feet barely feeling the circle of track. Once around the track was enough for Jan. Mrs. Krebs weeded out those needing to walk a few laps, then sent the rest of us on our way again, watching us like a hawk.

"Don't bounce, ladies!" she hollered. "Roll your foot. Heel to toe. Heel to toe."

"Don't bounce, ladies," Lacey mimicked.

"You're long-distance runners, not sprinters," called Mrs. Krebs. "Heel to toe."

"Heel to toe. Heel to toe," Lacey repeated in an affected British voice.

"Why don't you take the coach's advice?" I

suggested to her. "Then you won't look like a pogo stick."

Jessica, who was running next to us, turned her head to look at me with wide blue-green eyes, then stumbled a little. I passed the two of them, figuring they'd be gone by the third lap.

Lacey did join the walkers. But to my surprise Jessica was assigned another quick quarter of a mile with me and a few others.

"Take it back a few notches, Bethel," Coach told me before we started off. "I don't want you to pull a muscle."

I knew it was one of the dumbest things an athlete could do—show off and run too fast too soon.

Two more laps and the original group was down to just Jessica and me, Mary and Ginger. Krebsy looked pleased at our performance and had us slow down and join the others at a very slow jog.

We were halfway around the field from the coach when Lacey ran up behind Jan and began to imitate the way she moved. At first there was a surprised silence, then I saw the laughter bubbling up in Jessica and some of the other girls.

Grow up, I thought.

"Nice and steady, ladies," Mrs. Krebs called to us from across the field.

"Nice and steady, chubby," Lacey mimicked in an English accent.

Bethel

We were supposed to be cooling down, but I was heating up. Knowing how Mrs. Krebs handled kids in class, I was sure she wouldn't risk embarrassing Jan by correcting Lacey in front of the group. I gritted my teeth in anger. Not that I'm a good friend of Jan's—and not that I want her running in any of our meets—I'm not crazy! I've just seen this kind of stuff from Lacey one too many times.

"Jog tall," Mrs. Krebs encouraged us. "No need to look at your feet—they're still there."

"No need to look at your feet," Lacey continued in her stupid accent, "you can't see them anyway." Lacey kept on waddling awkwardly behind Jan, who pretended not to notice. Mary sped up to get by them. Unfortunately for Lacey, Mary stepped on her heel as she passed.

"Ow!" Lacey cried, and went sprawling forward. Flat on her face!

"Sorry," Mary said calmly, and kept on jogging.

I burst out laughing—I just couldn't help it. *Did she do that on purpose?* I wondered, but there was no way to be sure with Mary. Lacey glared up at me from the ground.

"You're so rude," Jessica said to me as two other girls helped Lacey to her feet.

"Well, at least when I laugh, I do it to somebody's face," I replied.

30

Jessica must have had *some* conscience—she blushed.

Jan acted like she hadn't even noticed the whole scene around her. She hates arguments.

Meanwhile Mrs. Krebs was sprinting across the field to us. Seeing that Lacey was okay, she slowed down. "All right, ladies," she said when she reached us, "we want to keep going—same pace, nothing faster. Baby those muscles. Keep it easy—we don't want any pulled hamstrings. Lacey," she said in a quieter voice, resting her hand on the girl's shoulder. "I think you've done enough today, don't you?"

Lacey gave Coach a snide smile, but she didn't argue. They walked off, and the group began to trot again. "You know," I whispered to Jessica as we jogged at the back of the group, "it's pretty mean to pick on other people because they're not in good shape. But it takes real nerve to do it when you aren't either."

Jessica's eyes flashed. "I could beat most of the guys in this school," she boasted.

"I wasn't talking about you," I said, my voice rising. "Though I have to admit, when I first saw you, I thought all you could do is build a human pyramid and shout, 'Rah! Rah!'"

I knew the red in her cheeks wasn't just from running.

31

"I'll take you on any day," Jessica challenged me, "in cheerleading *or* running."

For a moment the only sounds were light steps on the track and breathing. Everyone was listening to us.

"Let's start with running," I replied. "Down the track, around the water fountain, up the hill to the next field, around the goalpost and down again, finish by touching the bench." I pointed out the route as I spoke. "Backing down?" I asked when Jessica hesitated.

"On your mark," she answered me.

"Get set," I said.

"Go!" the others—even Jan—shouted.

We took off. Down the track we raced, elbow to elbow, our arms and feet in perfect rhythm. I quickened my pace. Jessica matched me. I had to take it up a notch higher if I wanted to pass her on the inside lane of the curving track. I accelerated again. So did she.

Well, Jessica Wakefield hadn't seen anything yet. I counted on the fact that she didn't have cross-country experience. Once we got off the track, she'd find things tougher. I led her by a yard or more when my feet touched the grass.

"Fountain!" I reminded her as we sprinted over the grass and weeds. The footing was tricky—uneven and wet. I cut the turn too tight, and my left foot slipped out from under me. Jessica, who was following me, quickly learned from my mistake and made up the distance. She was not only faster than I thought, she was smarter. We were neck and neck approaching the hill. *Not for long,* I thought.

"Yikes!" I heard her gasp as we started up.

I had run this hill before and knew it was steeper than it looked—like climbing a wall up to the next field. Stones slid out from under our feet where the path was eroded. Clumps of grass caught at our toes. Both of us went down on our knees, clawed at the hill with our hands, and scrambled up again.

We suddenly came over the top.

"Wait! Football practice!" Jessica exclaimed.

"What's the matter? You want to stop and do a few cheers?"

I didn't hesitate—just approached the field of players like an obstacle course. A moment later Jessica was sprinting next to me again. Whistles blew as we scooted through a play in the end zone. We cleared the goalpost. The last leg was coming up, and it was downhill.

Kids who don't run cross-country think downhill is the easy stuff. They take it too fast, which is just what Jessica did. She went skidding downward, like a skier out of control. She struggled to regain her footing and balance, and I picked up a yard on her.

When we hit the flat again, I knew she'd lose more. I've been there—legs all wobbly from the steep hill, your head kind of light. I charged for the finish line and touched the bench a good six yards ahead of her. A big cheer went up. The other girls had cut across the field to watch the finish of our race. Ginger and Bonnie ran over and slapped us both on the back, laughing.

"Way to go!" Ginger said.

Mary stood at the edge of the group. She looked directly at me, clapping quietly.

Unfortunately Mrs. Krebs wasn't clapping or laughing. In fact, she was looking grim, and I knew why. Racing was a stupid thing to do, and a disciplined athlete wouldn't have. Krebsy already warned us: A pulled muscle could put a runner out for days or weeks.

I bent over at my waist, tasting that funny iron taste down in my throat. Jessica paced in a small circle with her hands on her hips, breathing hard.

"Joggers, I'm really proud of your effort today," Krebsy said to the others. "You're off to a great start. Walk yourselves back to the locker room and make sure you drink plenty of water in the next hour. I'll see you here tomorrow."

Most of the girls glanced warily at Jessica and

me, knowing the coach wasn't happy with us, then walked back to the school building.

"You were great," Jan whispered as she passed me, then trotted after the others.

"Bethel, Jessica," Mrs. Krebs said, turning to us, "you have some cooling down to do, six laps for a start. I assume you were listening earlier and know why that wasn't a smart race to run."

We both nodded.

Krebsy made us walk in different directions so that we crossed paths twice each lap. By the last time around, I noticed that Jessica was limping a bit. I guess she was finally clueing in that I had been right about her shoes. Still—I could tell she was trying to act like her feet weren't hurting at all. Each time we met, I looked directly at Jessica and she met my gaze with steady blue-green eyes.

Stay clear of her, I thought. *Girls like her and Lacey are nothing but trouble, and they'll only drag the rest of us into it.*

Still—trouble or not—I had to admit Jessica Wakefield could run.

Wednesday, math class
Boring, boring, boring

Lacey,

Where were you yesterday? Practice was pretty good, but my feet are killing me. My leather shoes are worse than wearing platforms on a March of Dimes walk. I'm trying to get my parents to buy me running shoes. Work on your dad some, okay? Then I can say your dad's going to let you, and you can say my parents are going to let me, and we can shop together for them.

Jessica

Wednesday, Wilfred's class
Like you thought he'd be interesting?

Jessica,

I had stuff to do at the mall yesterday. Wish I'd known you needed shoes. Shoe-Be-Doo's had only one person working in the store, and the clerk kept disappearing in the back. Some good running shoes were sitting out, just asking to be stuffed in a backpack.

Lacey

Thursday morning

Hey, Lacey,

Does your stomach feel better today? Did you throw up? I'm sorry you felt sick at practice yesterday and had to leave so early. You missed running the trail through the woods. I called your house last night to find out how you were, but your stepmother said you weren't home.

Jessica

Thursday, Garbage-teria

Jessica,

I think it's this food that makes me want to throw up.

My wicked stepmother had me locked in the tower last night.

(Ha ha, she wishes.)

Don't call me—I'll call you.

Have fun at practice. I can't make it today either.

Lacey

Salvador

"Your grandmother is hanging swords from the dining-room chandelier?" Anna repeated as she unwrapped one of our cafeteria's famous barf burgers.

I glanced past her toward the door, where kids were streaming in for Friday's lunch. Still no sign of Elizabeth. "Yeah, sort of makes you sit up straight and keep your elbows off the table," I replied. "She says it's temporary, until she finds some space on the wall for them."

Anna nodded. She's spent a lot of time at my grandmother's, which is home for me while my parents work outside the States. So she knows my grandmother and her wackiness.

"The swords are a new hobby for the Doña," I went on with another quick glance at the door. Where was Elizabeth? "Thanks to fencing class." *Maybe Elizabeth is spending her lunch period in the library,* I thought. I wished she had told me—I would have gladly given up my slimy spaghetti to study with her.

"She's not here yet," Anna said.

"Who?" I asked.

She looked at me funny. "Elizabeth, who else?"

I think it's called "denial." I've heard the term on TV talk shows where people confess all kinds of strange things. I could never understand why you'd pretend someone wasn't important to you when really you thought that person was the greatest. Not until the first day of eighth grade, when I met Elizabeth.

Up till then, girls—except Anna, who doesn't count as a girl since she's my best friend—were something I enjoyed watching from across the room and teasing whenever I got the chance. But I didn't care what they thought of me or how they reacted to what I said. Not the way I cared and wondered with Elizabeth. And I couldn't seem to turn it off. I looked across the table at Anna and saw her staring down at her hamburger.

"I'm worried," she said, removing the roll from the top of her burger and using her knife to scrape off what might have been old shredded lettuce or slightly newer shredded onions. Like the spaghetti, it was slimy.

"I would be too, if I was going to eat that."

"Elizabeth was going down to the journalism

room," Anna continued, ignoring me, "to see if her Miss Perfect thing was accepted by the *Spectator*. It shouldn't have taken her this long to find out. I hope she didn't get bad news."

If you ask me, the *Spectator* *was* bad news. The paper was boring and stupid, and the editor was worse. But it had meetings that both Elizabeth and I went to. So once a week it was worth it.

"What if she's upset?" Anna said. "I wonder if I should check the girls' bathrooms."

"Better you than me," I told her. But then I saw Elizabeth hurrying in and waved her over. "Elizabeth!"

"Hi, Anna. Hi, Salvador," she said as I pulled out a chair for her. I hoped she noticed how gentlemanly I was being.

She smiled at both of us, like always. But her eyes weren't as bright as usual, and when she sat down, she hunched a little. There was a long silence, then she peeked at Anna and shook her head.

"No!" Anna said, her slim fist coming down hard, plunging her plastic knife straight into the hamburger. It oozed ketchup and some unidentifiable greenish stuff.

"You and my grandmother are getting dangerous," I told Anna.

Elizabeth managed to smile, but I could see she was faking it.

"No way—I just don't believe it," Anna said.

Elizabeth opened her lunch bag. "Well, Charlie did her best to explain why she—and the 'powers that be' as she calls them—rejected my piece."

"The powers that be?" Anna repeated, frowning.

"I guess she means the other editors. Anyway, someone else did a serious essay on student behavior beyond school property."

"So," I said, "that's perfect. Haven't Charlie and the Powers ever heard of presenting a topic through different points of view?"

"And," Anna added, "if the other essay was serious, a funny piece like yours would be a good complement to it."

"She didn't think it was funny. And Ted, the managing editor, said that a serious topic needs serious writing."

Anna rolled her eyes. "Since when is school-bus behavior a serious topic?"

"And they wonder why none of the students read the *Spectator*," I remarked.

"Actually, they don't wonder," Anna corrected me. "They assume everyone who doesn't read it is stupid and superficial. I heard the staff talking about it when I was doing some copy editing."

"I didn't know you were copy editing, Anna,"

Elizabeth said, then bit into her sandwich.

"Want some advice?" Anna replied, flicking her long, black hair over her shoulder. "Don't volunteer. The articles were so boring, I fell asleep between the sentences."

"I thought you were going to submit a poem," Elizabeth said.

Anna looked down at her plate. "I . . . uh . . . wasn't quite ready. The poems . . . need a little more work."

I had read some of Anna's poems. They didn't need work, but I hoped she wouldn't ever submit them. Anna acts tough, but I know she isn't. I didn't want Charlie and the Powers marking up her words or telling her they had something better to print.

"How about you, Salvador?" Elizabeth asked, turning to me.

Whenever she does that, suddenly gazing at me with her incredible blue-green eyes, I feel like someone has turned on a huge floodlight. I kept twirling my fork in the spaghetti, reluctant to suck up worms of it in front of her.

"Have you been working on some cartoons?" she asked.

I stared at Elizabeth's hands—the small dab of blue ink on her finger, the way the rope bracelet circled her wrist. "I submitted three of them yesterday, but—"

"I didn't know that." Anna sounded surprised.

I glanced up quickly. Lately I haven't been telling Anna all that I used to tell her, which was just about everything. I could never tell Anna what I think of Elizabeth, for example. I can't explain why. It's not like Anna would freak or something. But it would feel bizarre to talk about that.

"Yeah, well," I said to Anna, "I don't have a good feeling about getting accepted. Charlie said Mr. Lime is checking all art submissions for design and subject."

"Is that bad?" Elizabeth asked, looking from me to Anna.

"Mr. Lime is our art teacher," Anna explained. "He loves art, especially old paintings, historical works—"

"But doesn't get quite as excited about students," I finished for her.

Anna grinned. "Especially the kind who download a Great Masters painting from the Internet—a painting of a village celebration with a bunch of fat peasants—then use Photoshop to insert teachers' faces."

"I probably shouldn't have put it up on the school web site," I said.

"Or hung a copy on the bulletin board the day

the superintendent was visiting," Anna added.

Elizabeth laughed. "I'm surprised that Charlie even put you on the staff," she observed.

"My theory is that she likes to have a few people she can say no to," I replied. "It makes her feel smart."

Anna shook her head slowly. "She's so annoying," she murmured, more to herself than us. "Maybe we should—"

"What?" I asked when she broke off. I knew that expression—the way she pulled in her lower lip when she was thinking hard about something. "What are you thinking?"

She shrugged. "Nothing, really."

But the dark pools of her eyes said otherwise. That was my first hint that Anna wasn't telling *me* everything either.

"Jessica—It's Lacey, Saturday morning. You need a beeper—or at least your own message machine. Listen, something's come up, and I can't run with you today. I'll call you tomorrow."

Beep.

"Jessica—It's Lacey. Sunday. Why did you call me? I told you I'd call you. Don't act stupid. You'll get me in trouble. See you in school."

Beep.

Jessica

If I were back at Sweet Valley Middle school, at two-thirty on Monday afternoon, I'd be headed to cheerleading practice, swinging my shoes by their laces. Anybody who knew anything would know I had the coolest, most expensive pair of athletic shoes. But this was SVJH, and I was heading to cross-country practice—with sore feet. The heavy white leather felt like fifty pounds hanging from my hand.

Of course, I'd crawl into a hole and die before admitting to Bethel that she'd been right about my shoes. I was glad she couldn't hear me arguing with my parents at dinner every night. The conversation always went the same way, like a dumb TV repeat:

"Jessica, before you buy new shoes, let's wait and see if you really like running."

"I know I like it!"

"Let's see if you're still interested in it next week."

[*Hurt look*] "You don't believe me! My own parents don't believe what I say!"

"Sweetheart, we believe that you are enjoying the team this week."

[*Really hurt look, voice trembling*] "If my own family doesn't believe me . . ."

"You mean like we did when you played the piano for a week" [*Steven butting in*], "twirled a baton for a week, sewed half a skirt—"

Well, they'll be sorry when my feet are deformed for life, I thought, marching down the school hall past cafeteria tables piled with junk. *What's all this gross stuff?* I wondered.

A girl grabbed a sweater off the table. "I can't believe I never checked lost and found," she said, holding the sweater out to the girl next to her. "I lost this last year."

A sign advertised a sale. All the lost items that hadn't been claimed last year were being sold cheap. The sign hung directly above the head of a gray-haired man with a little mustache. I was pretty sure he was the art teacher, Mr. Lemon or Lime or Sour Grape or something.

His nose twitched, which made his mustache twitch, then he eyed a pair of shoes sitting on the table. *Maybe they smell,* I thought as I passed by.

Hey, wait a minute. I took a second look. Trainers! Running shoes, like Bethel's, only white—at least, they must have been when they were new. They looked about my size. Could I really deal with owning secondhand shoes?

Then again, could I really deal with wearing my uncomfortable ones even one minute longer?

I glanced around. Luckily only the nerds had stayed to sort through things. The nerd king— my locker partner, Ronald Rheece—was flipping through old textbooks. Like he didn't have enough already! All I needed was for him to call out in a loud, cheerful voice, "Jessica, what are you buying?" just as the football team went by on their way to practice. I hurried over to the mustached teacher.

"May I please see those shoes?" I whispered.

"What?" the man replied in a booming voice.

I felt like grabbing one of the rain ponchos and putting it on backward so the hood would cover my face. I raised my voice just a little and repeated the question.

"You'll have to pick them up yourself," the teacher replied. "I'm not touching them."

The fact that I did without stopping to think about it tells you how tired and cramped my feet were getting in their leather sneakers. I tried on one shoe, then the other. They were so comfy, so light, it felt like little wings were glued to my heels.

But never, ever in my life have I bought second-hand stuff. Somebody else's stuff, used-up stuff. Still, I really did like running, the shoes felt good, and the price was a dollar. The longer I took to decide, the more chance there was of someone who actually mattered walking by and seeing me.

I thrust a dollar in the hand of Mr. Lemon-Lime and took off. I headed for the girls' bathroom instead of the locker room. I had to make these things look like mine. It was bad enough to buy someone else's shoes, but I definitely couldn't walk around wearing them this way—what if someone recognized them?

Holed up in a stall, I pulled the purple laces from my leather shoes and threaded them through the trainers. Then I got out two fat, felt-tipped markers, purple and green, and went to work. The ink smeared on the nylon surface and my hands, but I managed to get hearts and stripes and—most important—my initials on the shoes. The color washed off my hands easily. I headed to the locker room.

I didn't know what I'd tell Lacey about the trainers. I was her only friend on the team, but I had a feeling that wouldn't stop her from making fun of my shoes. No matter how much I had tried to explain, Lacey just didn't get it—why I wouldn't steal a pair from Shoe-be-doo's.

Jessica

If she guessed I was wearing somebody else's shoes instead of helping myself to a pair like she did, I'd be humiliated. But each light step I took on the way to the locker room made me want to keep the shoes.

When I arrived, the other girls had already changed into their running outfits.

"Hi, Jessica," Jan greeted me. I couldn't believe how nice she always was. One time I had tried to tell her I was sorry—for that day that I didn't tell Lacey to stop making fun of her—but Jan waved off my apology. "No worries, Jessica," she said. "You barely even knew me then."

Well, that was changing . . . although it was changing rather slowly. Our group had shrunk to about fourteen kids. All of them were polite to me—they'd say hi in the hall. But they were cautious around me, especially when Lacey showed up. I understood how they felt. I mean, Lacey was my friend—well, sort of—but sometimes she scared even me.

Lacey was nowhere in sight. *I guess she's not coming—again.* Had Lacey gotten bored with running—or me?—I wondered idly as I pulled on my shorts. And why was she so snippy about me calling her? Did some friends, like her best bud, Kristin, have that privilege and others, like me, have to wait for her to call? And was Lacey ever going to introduce me to Splendora?

"We'll tell Mrs. Krebs you're here, Jessica," Ginger said as the girls started toward the door.

"Hey," Jan said, "somebody forgot a jacket."

"Bethel!" Lana called down the hallway. "Your jacket. And while you're at it, get your stinky old socks away from my locker."

"How do you know they're mine?" Bethel asked, coming back into the locker room, her eyes sweeping the floor.

I quickly pulled my feet under the bench where I was sitting, trying to make them less noticeable.

"Who else leaves behind a trail of clothes and notebooks?" Lana replied.

"True," Bethel admitted, then stooped to pick up her socks. "Hey!"

I concentrated on braiding my hair, hoping that Bethel wasn't staring at my feet when she said that. She was, and now so was everyone else.

"Different shoes," Bethel observed, her dark eyes shining.

If only she had said *new* shoes.

"Yeah," I replied, trying to sound casual. "I found my old trainers in the back of my closet."

"Really?" Bethel said, coming closer so she could see them better. "They look a lot like *my* old trainers."

Hers? They couldn't be! But then, with all

those things she kept leaving behind—some of them were sure to end up in lost and found. Just my luck—the same luck I'd been having since I started at this stupid school.

"An *awful* lot like my shoes," Bethel added.

"Well, I guess we like the same kind," I told her.

Bethel gave me a long look. I met it, determined not to look away first. *You can't intimidate me,* I thought.

"We sure don't like the same colors," she said, then walked away.

The others followed her outside to the track.

I leaned over, resting my arms on my knees, staring down at my shoes. Had I convinced Bethel? *No way,* I thought, *she's too smart.* We'd pretty much stayed away from each other since that first practice, but I could tell that Bethel still didn't like me.

But if that was true—then why had she just cut me a break?

The New, Cost-cutting School Lunch Menu

by Elizabeth Wakefield

Monday	Tuesday	Wednesday
Green-cheese sandwich on rock-hard roll	Italian special: noodles & ketchup	Rubber burger
Chicken soup, chicken removed	Deflated peas	Fries with extra grease
Re-re-refried beans	Squash	Limp-crust pizza with pepperoni & oil pools

Thursday	Friday
Make your own combo:	Something under thick gravy
Chicken fingers	Something under thick cheese sauce
Sausage toes	
Meatless ribs	Dessert special: something under ice cream
with Elmer's glue rice	
	An extra serving for anyone who can guess what something is

Anna

I stared down at the paper headed
Memo to Anna. It had been left in my mailbox
in the *Spectator* office early Friday morning:

"Anna," Charlie wrote in a fat blue pencil,
"please look very carefully at the attached, i.e.,
the article you copyedited and the final version,
which I had to correct. In the future, submit
clean copy only, i.e., work that does not have to
be rechecked by me. When necessary, consult a
grammar book. Please do not split infinitives."

As I headed down the hall to Elizabeth's
locker, I glanced over "the attached." In a boring
six-page article on school spirit, which had been
full of run-on sentences, mixed tenses, incorrect
spellings, and fragments, I had overlooked one
phrase: "to really try." One phrase! I was ready
to spit infinitives—in Charlie's face. *That's it,* I
thought. *I'm gone.*

"Anna . . . Anna?"

I looked over my shoulder. I had walked right

past Elizabeth's locker. I turned around and tossed the stupid memo and article in a hallway trash can. See ya later, *Spectator.*

"Hey, Elizabeth," I said, turning to her. "Good news?"

"I don't know," she replied quietly. "I haven't checked yet."

Elizabeth had written another parody, this time setting up a cafeteria menu like the one they posted each week on the bulletin board. Hers, however, came a lot closer to the truth than the official lunch plan. I thought it was great, but she was nervous about it.

"I was thinking about dropping by the journalism room before class this morning," Elizabeth said.

"Want me to go along?" I asked. Yesterday afternoon she had rejected Salvador's offer to do the same. I guess sometimes it's weird to hang with a guy you don't know very well. Maybe that's why she'd said no. Still, Salvador had looked hurt, as if Elizabeth had told him he smelled gross or something. I didn't want her to think I'd get all freaky on her like Sal did. "I'll totally understand if you want to go by yourself."

"No, come with me," Elizabeth said, tugging a piece of her blond hair.

She shifted her books from one arm to the

other. I could tell she was nervous. It seemed all wrong to me that someone with real writing talent could have her confidence blown by a girl like Charlie.

"Just remember," I told her, "if they reject this one, which everyone in this school would think is hilarious, they really don't know what they're doing." I know this is mean, but in a weird way I hoped they *would* reject it. Then it would be easy to talk Elizabeth and Salvador into quitting the paper with me.

"Maybe."

We walked down to the first floor in silence.

I wished I could think of something to say—something that would make Elizabeth less nervous. My brother was always good at that. So not fair. Didn't he and I have the same parents? You would never know it. Things never bothered him the way they bother me. Like, he would never consider quitting the *Spectator.* He would just charm Charlie until she printed whatever he wanted.

"Okay, take a deep breath," I told Elizabeth as we entered the journalism room.

"Hello, girls," Charlie said, sounding like somebody's mother. A coffee mug sat on her desk, its rim stained with dark lipstick. "How are you? Anna, did you get my memo?"

"Yes," I replied. "I've already filed it. Hi, Ted."

"Hi," the ninth-grader greeted us in a softer, shyer voice. He was sitting at one of the long tables that ran around the rim of the room. He's the managing editor and so serious about things, he makes me seem like a stand-up routine on The Comedy Channel.

"I, uh, came by to see if you had a chance to read my submission," Elizabeth said.

"Yes, we did," Charlie replied, circling words on the paper in front of her and scribbling a note at the top. "Ted," she said, without looking at him or us, "would you like to give your assessment?"

"Uh . . ." Ted touched his horn-rimmed glasses with smooth brown hands, then touched them again, as if he couldn't set them quite right. I had a feeling he'd rather Charlie did the talking. "It was different from anything we've received at the *Spectator*," Ted said carefully.

"Well, did you take it or didn't you?" I demanded.

"Sorry," Charlie said. "Pink slip."

In other words, a rejection. Why couldn't she just say yes or no like everyone else?

"No problem," Elizabeth told them graciously.

"Well, I have a problem," I said, taking a step closer to Charlie's desk and putting my hands flat on the paper she was trying to edit. "I thought it was great, just like her piece on school-bus etiquette. It made a point and was funny. What else could you want for the paper?"

Charlie sat back. "I'm afraid we cover more important topics than school lunch."

"I'd say lunch is pretty important to most kids in this school," I countered.

Charlie spread out her hands and gave a little shrug. "Well, I'm not responsible for the intellectual quality of the students here."

Elizabeth gave me a let's-get-out-of-here look. I couldn't believe it! Wasn't she going to stand up for herself? Was she just going to agree with a stuck-up girl whose brain was smaller than the cafeteria's deflated peas?

Ted studied his hands. He had been in a music class with me, and I knew he was smart. Why did he put up with Charlie? Was he that desperate to work on the stupid newspaper? Well, I wasn't.

"There is another problem," Charlie added. "The food service was chosen by the principal and the head of the PTA. We don't want to ruffle any feathers."

"Especially since the PTA raises money for the paper," I remarked. *That's honest,* I thought sarcastically. *You give us money and we'll write whatever you want to hear.*

"There is a topic we could use a good piece on,"

Ted interjected in a soothing voice. "Elizabeth, I'd love to see something from you on ecology."

Charlie nodded her approval. "Now that's something people need to hear about. And perhaps it will inspire you to consider other hard-hitting social issues that would be worth writing about. You too, Anna," she said cheerfully.

"No thanks," I told her.

Charlie cocked an eyebrow.

"I quit." I turned and walked out of the room. Lockers flew by as I stormed down the hall.

Elizabeth ran after me. "Anna!" she called. I turned and waited for her to catch up. "I can't believe you just did that!" she whispered.

"Why not? Why would I want to work with a bunch of worm brains?" I said, disgusted. "They stick their little heads in the dirt and wonder why everybody else sees things in a brighter light."

Elizabeth shook her head. "They rejected me, not you, Anna."

That's right! I thought. *You should care too!* But I just said, "It's more than that, Elizabeth." I gripped my books so hard, the spiral spines bit into my fingers. "They're not honest journalists. They write whatever the PTA and the principal want to read," I said.

Elizabeth nodded quietly.

"Well, doesn't that bother you?"

"Yes," she admitted.

"Enough to quit?" I asked.

Elizabeth stared at me. "Quit?"

"Why not? I just did. We have better things to do with our time than work for people like Charlie and Ted," I said. We stepped around a group of ninth-graders sitting on the floor, playing cards by someone's locker. "I mean, despite the awards, do you really think they're doing good stuff?"

She shook her head.

"So do you want to be part of a paper like that?"

Elizabeth bit her lip. "Do you think Salvador will quit?"

What did *that* have to do with anything? Didn't she understand what I was saying about the *Spec*? "I don't know what Salvador's going to do. He isn't excited about Mr. Lime checking the art, but he still wants to submit cartoons. You know Salvador—he needs an audience."

Elizabeth glanced away. I had a sudden pang— *What if the two of them stay on the paper without me?* I pushed that thought away. *They won't.*

"Just because he wants to do it," I added, "doesn't mean you have to."

She nodded again. But she didn't answer.

It's only a matter of time, I told myself. *She'll quit. Salvador too.*

After all—those two had absolutely no good reason to stay on the *Spec*. Especially not without me.

                              Friday
                      Typing c;ass
Jesssica ,
   If Krebz gives out teeam shirts
today, take One for me/
   And find out wjat time we get out
of c;ass Monday, I mean
   for the meett. I told tje old witch
and my father that I'm spending
   Saturday witj you, so don't call my
house/ I'll talk to you Sundau.
                              Lacey

Bethel

"All right, ladies, last lap. Take it slow," Krebsy called to us from across the field.

I love running in the rain. Wind is even better. During Friday's practice the rain was light, but the wind was great, gusting up in our faces, trying to hold us back like a wall.

"Do you think she's going to tell us today or wait till Monday?" Lana asked as we warmed down. Her short, blond hair stood up in the breeze like wisps of straw. She had been working hard and really wanted to run in the meet Monday. But she wasn't exactly speedy.

"Mrs. Krebs has to tell us today," Ginger said. "She wouldn't make us wonder all weekend."

Jessica jogged silently, staring at her feet. Good thing I hadn't made any bets on the chance of her coming to every practice—I would have lost big time. Of course, Lacey had missed about two-thirds of the workouts in the last two weeks, just like she was missing today's. The only surprise there was that she had come to any.

"Good show today," Krebsy said as the pack of us arrived back at the bench. "Good show all week! Take a seat, please."

We did quickly. Mrs. Krebs tugged on her long, brown braid and studied her clipboard.

I bent over, resting my elbows on my legs, dropping my head a little, studying all the nervous feet dancing under the bench. Every time I looked at Jessica's, I felt like laughing. The only closet she could have dug those running shoes out of was mine. My big toes always wear through the top of my shoes in a certain way, so I recognized the trainers the first day she showed up with them, in spite of their disguise.

It was starting to rain harder, and Mrs. Krebs turned over her clipboard to keep the papers dry. She smiled at us. "We could chat inside," she said in her cheerful British voice, "but it's been dry for two weeks, and I want you to get used to the rain. Meets go on rain or shine, you know, and you can't run a race with a brolly—an umbrella," she translated for us.

As if some Olympic god had overheard our coach, the skies suddenly opened up. It poured. We shifted in our places, trying to look like the rain didn't bother us. Ginger's red bangs were

Bethel

hanging straight down in her eyes. Bonnie's thin
T-shirt clung to her amazing boobs, which we'd
all agreed were a big advantage in crossing the
finish line first. Puddles were quickly forming
around our feet. I noticed Jessica's feet again.
The green and purple ink on the shoes was running. What a mess! I let out a little snort, and
Jessica glared at me. What was she so worried
about? We all looked terrible—who cared?

"It's just water," Krebsy said, laughing. "Now,
as I told you last week, our first meet involves six
schools. This early in the season none of us have
full squads ready to compete in a 3K race, so the
other coaches and I have decided to run just five
girls each. More of you will be participating in
later meets. Every girl who works hard on this
team will get her chance to run. All right?"

I nodded. Rain ran off my nose and ears and
soaked my shorts. The green-and-purple mess of
Jessica's shoes was bleeding into her socks.

"So here's the lineup for Monday," Coach said.
"Mary Stillwater, Bethel—"

I'd figured we'd make it.

"Jessica, Ginger."

Them too.

"And Lana," she added.

Lana?

I saw Jessica turn around quickly to glance at

Lana. Jody was faster than Lana, but she'd missed a few times. And Lacey, when she tried, was faster than both of them.

"Everyone here gets a shirt," Mrs. Krebs said. She pulled open a soggy box full of plastic bags, each with a team shirt inside it, purple and white for our school colors. "Medium and large. Come and get them."

"What? No small?" Jan joked. She had told us last week that her real reason for joining the team was to lose weight—and that she'd already lost four pounds.

We all started laughing and talking and tossing shirts to each other. All of us except Jessica, that is, who stood there running her fingers through her wet hair like a comb.

"I was just wondering," I heard her say to Mrs. Krebs, "did you forget about Lacey?" I rolled my eyes.

"Lacey Frells? No, I didn't forget her."

"What I mean is"—Jessica glanced sideways at Lana—"Lacey's pretty fast. Faster than some people."

"She's missed seven out of ten practices, Jessica," Krebsy replied. "If she wants to run with us, she has to earn her place on the team."

"Well, I'm sure she'll start coming again," Jessica said.

Don't hold your breath, I thought.

"I look forward to that," Coach answered.

"So I'll take a shirt for her too," Jessica added, quickly reaching into the carton.

What? No way was Lacey getting a shirt—not if I had anything to say about it. I was about to speak up, but Krebsy rested a light hand on Jessica's arm. "If Lacey decides to become a regular, I'll make sure she gets a shirt."

Jessica gave Mrs. Krebs a sulky pout. It might have been effective with some people, but it ran off our coach like the rain. *Jessica Wakefield, you better check yourself,* I thought. *I don't know what your friend is after, but she's not getting it on my team.*

Krebsy closed up the box and turned to the rest of us. "Don't forget your light workouts over the weekend. I want everyone shirted up Monday. Those of you not competing will still be doing warm-ups and assisting along the course. I'll submit the names of all of you here to the office so you're eligible for early dismissal. See you then."

As we headed back to the locker room, I caught up with Jessica. I'd been trying to avoid her in general, but I couldn't resist messing with her after she'd tried to steal a shirt for Lacey. "Nice shoes," I said. "Nice socks."

She lifted her chin, ignoring me.

"The green especially. But stay clear of Miss Scarlett," I warned. Everyone knew that our gym teacher had a thing about bacteria growing on feet. "If she sees them, you'll be quarantined."

Ginger, who was walking in front of us, glanced over her shoulder and laughed. Even Mary, whose face was often as still as her last name, smiled.

Jessica just shrugged.

"If I were you," I continued, "I'd take them back to the store where you bought them and complain."

She said nothing.

"I hope you didn't pay a lot for them."

Jessica just kept walking.

Where did you say you got them? I was about to challenge her, but then I saw her blinking. Was she . . . was she *crying*? I felt a sudden stab of guilt.

Maybe it was just the rain. I mean, girls like her don't have feelings that get hurt. They're too snobby for that. Right?

But I had been wrong about her sticking it out and running hard every day. Maybe I didn't know Jessica as well as I thought.

I decided to leave her alone.

Just in case.

Jessica

"Jess! Hey, Jess—want a ride?" my brother shouted at me through the car window he had just rolled down. "You look like a drowned rat!"

"I'd rather drown than be seen with you," I hollered back, and stalked on. He drove off.

Actually, it was kind of nice of him to offer, but I could make a better entrance by walking the last half block home from the bus stop and stomping into the kitchen soaked. I'd let my stupid, ugly shoes bleed green and purple all over the floor. Maybe my family would notice then that life wasn't exactly great for me.

"Hey," Dad greeted me a few minutes later when I came in the door, "look what just waddled in from the pond."

"Hi, Jessica," Mom said, her head stuck in a kitchen cupboard. "Dry off fast, okay? We're having an early dinner tonight."

So much for instant sympathy and disbelief at

the horrible shoes I was forced to wear. Why was I surprised? When I'd first come home with the secondhand trainers, my parents had been shocked. Shocked and *happy*.

"Now I *know* you love running," Mom had said.

Dad had smiled. "You've come up with a great solution, Jessica." But—*hello*—neither one of them had gotten the hint that they were supposed to be impressed with my dedication and *buy me new shoes*.

Tonight was my last chance to get them before my first meet.

At least Elizabeth hadn't left for her *Spectator* meeting yet. I could always count on my twin to feel sorry for me. "I thought this was newspaper night," I said.

"This week the meeting is only for the powers that be—the important editors," she replied as she set the big farm table we have in our kitchen. "How was practice?"

"Wet."

She smiled.

"*Very* wet," I added, looking down at my trainers so she would.

"Wow, look at your shoes and socks," Elizabeth said, and began to laugh. "Tie-dyed."

"Doesn't anyone in this house *care?*" I exploded.

My mother pulled her head out of the cupboard.

69

My father stopped stirring the pot on the stove. Elizabeth paused before she laid down the next spoon. All of them stared at me. Steven, who had just entered the kitchen from the living room, said, "Well, I offered you a ride home."

"That's not what I'm talking about!" I snapped.

"Did something happen today, sweetheart?" Mom asked.

"Today?" I almost screamed. "Not just today. Try every day this week and every day the week before."

My parents exchanged puzzled looks. Nothing is worse than parents who don't get it. It's almost impossible to make them feel bad for you.

"Is it the shoes?" Elizabeth guessed.

"Gee, why would you think that?" I asked. "I just love wearing these disgusting things. I love having the other girls on my team stare at my hand-me-down shoes."

This time my parents exchanged knowing looks. Not a good sign.

"Congratulate me," I went on. "I'm one of the five girls chosen to run in the meet on Monday and I've got to wear *these*. I can't wait till the runners from the other teams see them and laugh. How am I supposed to deal with *that*?"

"Make them your trademark," Steven suggested.

"You know, act like it's cool and everyone will think it is."

I couldn't believe he'd said that. "You make that fat old Buick your trademark," I told him. "That ugly gray car that ninety-year-old Mr. Hanson was going to give you for almost nothing. Then see how cool you feel cruising around in it."

Steven shut up quick.

"Did a teammate say something to you about your shoes?" Elizabeth asked me gently.

I flopped down in a kitchen chair as dramatically as I could. "You just don't know how humiliating it's been, how totally and completely humiliating." (Okay, so I was exaggerating— sometimes you have to play things up to win an argument.) I took a shaky breath. "For two weeks I've had to wear these soggy, smelly things with their ugly, runny colors. They're so wet, I can't untie them anymore." I wrenched one shoe off my foot and dangled it from its knotted shoestring.

"But today is the first day it's rained in two weeks," Steven pointed out.

I glared at him.

"Jessica," my mother said, "we have discussed new shoes several times in the past two weeks. I thought you understood our reasons for not buying a pair right away."

Jessica

I understood enough to know I couldn't win this argument if we got into reasoning. "Mom," I said, "remember when you bought that expensive briefcase and portfolio and you weren't sure if you should and Dad said definitely do it? He said you needed them so others would know you're professional. Well, I'm one of five people running in a real meet. I need good shoes if I want to be professional." I gave her a pleading look. "And a few new pairs of shorts, and some new tank tops, and a warm-up suit," I added hopefully.

"The difference is that when your mother bought the portfolio, she had been a decorator for more than two weeks," Dad pointed out. "Besides, there's nothing wrong with the shoes you've got."

I scowled and stood up. I'd have to try another tactic. "Well, I guess what they say about girls and sports is true."

Steven took my bait. "What do they say?"

"That people still don't take girl athletes seriously. It's a proven fact. Girls' sports never get the same funding as boys' do. And parents don't—like—support it as much when their daughters do sports."

My father simply raised his eyebrows. I should have realized a women's-rights argument wouldn't convince a dad who does most of the cooking and half of the laundry, especially when he was Mom's biggest fan when she was all-American in college sports.

"Jessica, you remember, don't you," my mother said quietly, "that you spent your entire clothes budget on a purple kilt that you wore one day, the first day of school, and never again?"

"Why do you have to keep bringing that up?" I cried.

"And," she went on calmly, "Steven and Elizabeth agreed afterward that we all make mistakes, so Dad and I gave you extra money to buy a few more things, which means that you received more than Steven or Elizabeth this fall."

I paced around the kitchen table. "Yeah, but you gave Lizzie a computer. Her own computer in her room so she can write stuff for the paper."

Elizabeth's cheeks got pink. "That's not true—it's yours too," she said. "And you were the one who said I could keep it in my room. Besides, the computer is secondhand, just like the shoes."

I stared at her in shock. What a traitor! Would it have killed her to help me win this argument? "Nobody understands! Nobody really cares what it's like for me at this stupid new school!" I picked up the plate and silverware from my usual place at the table and handed them to my sister. "I'm not hungry!" I said, then stomped up to my room. Which wasn't easy to do since I was wearing only one shoe.

When I got to my bedroom, I yanked off my other shoe, threw it across the room, and lay back on my quilt, staring at the ceiling for a while. Nobody had followed me upstairs. I figured I was stuck with the ugly trainers. Could I turn the dumb old shoes into something cool, like Steven suggested? Maybe I could if I were back at Sweet Valley Middle School, but that seemed like a previous lifetime of mine.

Downstairs in the kitchen, I could hear laughter and dishes clattering. The smell of Dad's creamy vegetable pasta and warm bread floated up to my room. My stomach growled. *I can't believe I'm skipping dinner and they don't even care,* I thought. I got up and took a long, long shower so I wouldn't have to keep sniffing dinner. I put a special conditioner on my hair and sat there in the steam, thinking how awful my family would feel if I ended up going to the Olympics or something. "I would like to thank no one but myself for winning this gold medal for my country," I said to the mirror. I painted my toenails purple and white for good luck on Monday. When I finally emerged from the bathroom, I saw Mom sitting on my bed. For a moment neither of us said anything, then she patted the space next to her. "Want to talk?"

I wasn't sure, but I sat down.

"I like the toes," Mom said.

"Mom, did you ever think that you probably don't deserve something, and you're arguing for it in dumb ways and acting like a brat, but you just really, really want it anyway?"

"Yes, about once a week," my mother replied.

I had to laugh.

"Jessica, I want to make sure you understand why Dad and I aren't rushing out to get you these shoes. One reason is that you change your mind a lot. Another is that we try to divide equally what we have among the three of you. We love you all very much—we can't give more to one than to the others. And as far away as it may seem now, we do need to save for three college tuitions."

I nodded.

"So, here's what Dad and I propose. Tomorrow you and I will go to the runners' store at the mall and find you a good pair of shoes. Dad and I will pay for them now, but you will earn back their cost by doing extra work around the house. We'll keep a tab because we think it's important for you to become responsible for your expenses. How's that sound?"

"Good," I said. "Great!" I couldn't wait to go shopping! I wanted to run out right away. *You*

can wait twelve hours, I told myself. *Calm down.*
"Thanks, Mom," I whispered, hugging her.

"Whoa," she said, laughing, "you're squishing the brownies!" She pulled a folded square of napkin from her pocket. "Elizabeth rescued these for you before Steven finished off the pan. There's also some terrific pasta downstairs waiting to be microwaved, if you're hungry enough for dinner."

"I'm starved! And I have to make sure I eat healthy this weekend so I'm ready to race."

"Oh, well, if you're eating healthy," Mom said, trying to take back the brownies. She loves chocolate as much as I do.

"Like you've said before, Mom," I replied, holding on to my dessert, "chocolate's a bean, and you know how good beans are for you."

Dear Diary,

Unbelievable. Things are working out even better than I thought. Daddy is so proud of the fact that I'm "getting into sports." He thinks it will look good on a college application. What a joke.

Kristin is always busy with cheer squad.

Even Jessica has stopped bothering me about coming to practice.

Nobody ever asks where I am after school anymore.

Lacey

News Release
by Salvador del Valle

The Bored of Education has recently proposed school uniforms for junior-high-school students. If passed, the students will be able to choose from three uniform looks. Internationally unknown designer Salvador del Valle has submitted the following styles to the Bored.

The Retro Uniform

While this style is now available at the mall, we will accept only a certified pair of Sonny Bono bell-bottoms and vest for both boys and girls. Students will have a choice of colors for headbands and love beads—psychedelic orange, green glow, and Aquarius purple. Heavy socks (must match headbands) may be worn under sandals in colder weather.

The Preppo Uniform

For the sophisticated student we offer pants and skirts in beige and khaki. Our button-down shirts made of cotton have refined stripes and come in all colors currently available for a sports-utility vehicle. Only expensive loafers may be worn with this uniform. Especially recommended for the Harvard bound.

The Nerdo Uniform

For the true individualist we offer an easy-to-care-for uniform of polyester. For the young man we have pants that hitch up two inches above the natural waistline and a shirt not even his father would wear. For the young lady a blouse with a little round collar and a skirt that turns on her waist so that the zipper is always in the wrong place. Baggy panty hose is required beneath these skirts. The young man will be able to choose between nylon socks in blue, black, and blue-black. Any shoe that squeaks may be worn.

A n n a

I was laughing so hard, I bumped my nose on the scoops of ice cream towering above my cone, which made Salvador laugh too. He tossed a napkin at me. I wiped off a glob of Jazzberry, the Saturday special at Farrelly's, careful not to let any of it drip on Salvador's latest idea for the *Spectator,* which was right in front of me.

For a year now our county school board had been debating the pros and cons of having a school uniform, getting people all worked up about individual rights and the styles we'd have to wear. I read Salvador's suggestions three times, laughing each time at the drawings and his "fashion voice."

"You like it," he said, sounding happy and even grateful.

"It's terrific. I think I'll wear retro."

"Do you really, honestly think it's good?" he persisted, then quickly licked a chocolate drip.

We both took a moment to catch up with our melting ice cream.

"It will be the best thing the *Spectator* has ever printed," I predicted. *Not that there's much competition in that category,* I added silently. I hadn't had a chance to tell Salvador that I'd quit yet—but this looked like a good opening. I opened my mouth, but Sal cut me off.

"Don't count on it," he said.

"What do you mean?" I crunched down on a piece of cone.

"It's already been rejected."

I shook my head. "*That* figures. Wait till I tell Elizabeth—"

"I don't want her to know," he interrupted quickly.

What? I sat back in my chair. "Why not?" I asked.

"I don't know. . . ." He fiddled with his napkin. "I'm just not comfortable with her the way I am with you."

I smiled, then looked down at the table. A warm feeling spread through my body. I don't know why, but it made me feel good to know that I was number one with Salvador. *That'll never change,* I thought.

"It's the paper that stinks, not you," I assured him. I looked up from the table. "Salvador," I said quietly, "I quit."

His eyebrows flew up. "You quit the paper?" he asked. "Why didn't you tell me?"

"You left school early to go to that fencing tournament with the Doña, remember?" I said. "I called last night, but you were still out, so I just figured I'd tell you today."

He shook his head. "You finally got me to *join* the *Spectator* and now you've quit?"

"I didn't know it would be as bad as it was," I protested. "The stories I copyedited this week were so boring, they made Mr. Wilfred's math class seem like a nonstop thrill ride. If that was the only kind of writing they got, I'd understand. But they've rejected stuff from Elizabeth and you that's really good. Even if—"

"Have you told Elizabeth?" he interrupted, leaning forward a little, his elbows on the table.

"—even if you did get something published by the *Spectator*," I continued, trying to keep the irritation out of my voice, "who's going to read it except the people giving out journalism awards at the Board of Education?"

"Have you told Elizabeth that you've quit?" he asked a second time.

I rolled my eyes. "She was there when I did it."

"What did she say?"

"She agrees with me," I told him. "She thinks

they publish lousy, boring articles. And she knows they'll write whatever the principal and the PTA want to see."

Salvador wrinkled his forehead in confusion. "But is she going to quit?" he asked finally.

I ran my finger along the smooth edge of the marble table. "I'm pretty sure she will." Why did Salvador and Elizabeth only seem to care what the other was going to do? Didn't it matter what *I* wanted to do?

"So—are *you* going to quit?" I asked.

"I don't know," he said flatly.

What? I couldn't believe it! How could he stay on the paper when I'd quit? The *Spec* was awful—he had to know that. So what was keeping him there?

Was it—could it be—Elizabeth?

"If you stare at that table any harder, you'll burn a hole in it," Salvador said.

"I was thinking."

"No kidding," he said.

"All finished?" I asked him.

"No, I'm hiding my ice cream in my pocket."

For once Salvador's joke irritated me instead of making me laugh. I scraped back my chair. He stood up with me.

"So you're not going to tell me what you're thinking about?"

"I don't have to tell you everything, Salvador,"
I said coldly.

He studied me for a moment, his head tilted
to one side. "You used to." He picked up his
folder as I turned to leave the shop and followed
me out into the main part of the mall.

In front of the sporting-goods store, Salvador
suddenly tugged on my shirt. Not ten feet in
front of us, peering into the store window, were
a pretty blond woman and her pretty blond
daughter. "It's Jessica," I whispered to him.

"How can you tell without seeing her face?"

How could he *not* tell? "Her clothes. Her atti-
tude. The way she walks." Sometimes I think
guys are blind.

Jessica suddenly turned and faced us. "Hi,
Anna. Hey, El Salvador."

Mrs. Wakefield turned. "Hello," she said with
a smile that dazzled like her daughters'.

"Hi," I said, and Salvador mumbled something. I hoped he wasn't going to start acting
odd around all of the Wakefields now.

"We're buying sneakers," Mrs. Wakefield said.

Jessica rolled her eyes. "They're *trainers,* Mom,"
she said. "See you guys in school," she said to us,
and strode into the store. Mrs. Wakefield gave us
a small shrug and followed her daughter.

"It's strange to see different versions of

Elizabeth, don't you think?" Salvador asked me, staring after them.

"Elizabeth is the best version," I said. I meant it too, even if I did wish Salvador found me and my plans as interesting as he seemed to find her. Why did he care so much about her? Had I just gotten boring or something?

"What are you thinking?" he asked. "You've been so quiet lately, quieter than usual."

"I'll tell you what's on my mind," I challenged, "if you tell me what's on yours."

He looked uncomfortable. "Oh, you know me," he said, "completely mindless."

"That's what I figured," I replied.

Salvador laughed, but he didn't say anything else. And neither did I.

Elizabeth

I had to give it one more try. Maybe the article would seem better this time.

I understood why Anna quit the paper, but I just wasn't ready to give up Friday nights with Salvador yet. I nestled into the crook of the big pine tree in our backyard and stared down at the typed sheets clipped to my writing pad. After talking to Charlie and Ted, I had started writing an ecology article in the *Spectator* style. I stayed late after school to work on it and left it on Charlie's desk on Friday, but I hadn't told Anna or Salvador about it. I didn't want them to ask to see it—it was too, too lame.

I read the article again just to make sure it was as bad as I thought.

Next to Sweet Valley Junior High is a stream that was once clean. Now cans protrude from the muddy bank and trash floats in the water. Whose responsibility is this? Ours. Who is responsible for the world in the twenty-first century? We are.

If you are concerned that . . .

This is nauseating, I thought, unclipping the article and hiding it at the bottom of my writing pad. Why did I keep trying? *SALVADOR*, I wrote in big, script letters on the yellow pad. *Salvador del Valle,* I wrote smaller.

"Hi, Lizzie!"

I glanced toward the back door of our house and quickly ripped off the top sheet, slipping it under my article. Jessica came bounding toward me.

"Hey, look, it's a gazelle," I said.

Jessica grinned.

She looked like a model in one of the ads she had clipped out of Steven's magazine, her hair pulled into a golden braid, her eyes as bright as the fall sky.

"Put your foot up here—let me see," I said when she was standing in front of the tree.

With the flexibility of a ballerina, my twin propped one foot up on the trunk. The shoe was made of lavender nylon with a thin strip of leather on each side. Its sole looked like a black rubber waffle.

"No guy is ever going to catch you now," I teased.

"Don't worry, I know when to slow down," she replied, laughing. "Look." She twisted her foot around. "This is the most important part. It's cushioned to protect my heel when I land and rounded so I can roll forward on my foot."

"Are trainers like normal shoes? Do you have to break them in?"

"Not as much," she replied. "Krebsy told us to get some z's and do easy workouts this weekend, which will be just enough to break them in."

Krebsy? Get some z's? My sister the cheerleader was starting to talk like a jock. She suddenly dropped down on the grass beneath the tree and began to do stretches, the kind Steven did when he warmed up for a run.

"I see you laughing," she said, peeking up at me.

"I'm *smiling*," I told her. "You look really cool—in shape and cool. Do you have a schedule for the team? I'd like to see a race, and I bet Anna and Salvador would too."

"I'll ask for one Monday and hang it on the fridge," she said, pulling her right foot back and bending her knee at a sharp angle. "By the way, I saw Anna and El Salvador at the mall."

"You did?"

"Coming out of Farrelly's," she said, keeping her left leg straight out in front of her and bending forward to touch her toe. "El Salvo looked kind of funny when I turned around and saw him."

"Funny how?" I asked. Why hadn't Anna and Salvador invited me out with them? *They've been friends for a long time,* I reminded myself. *Naturally they still do stuff together.* They didn't have to ask me along every time. So why did I feel so left out?

"Just funny," Jessica replied after switching legs. "I mean, funny's pretty normal for Salvador, isn't it?" she added with a sly smile.

I shrugged, then bit my lip. "What's with the smile?" I asked. She grinned even wider. "Stop looking at me like that!"

When Jessica had finished that exercise, she stood up. "Do you like him, Elizabeth?"

"Of course I like him. We're friends."

"Okay, okay. Somebody's kind of touchy today," Jessica said. She was still grinning.

Jessica would just keep bugging me if I let her. "What are you doing now?" I asked, changing the subject.

She had placed her palms against the pine tree, right below where I was sitting. Her feet were planted apart. She leaned forward, pushing against the tree with all her weight, keeping her heels flat on the ground.

"Trying to push your tree over," she said. "You don't mind, do you?"

Elizabeth

I shook my head. "Not as long as you pick it up again." Jessica did several more stretches. "Okay, I'm out of here," she announced, and sprinted off.

I watched as she disappeared around the house, then rested my head back against the pine tree, thinking. Had Anna asked Salvador to go for ice cream, or had Salvador asked her? As fast as that question popped into my mind, I pushed it out. It shouldn't make any difference to me which one did the inviting.

What are you? I asked myself. *Jealous?*

Lacey

Gel and I were cruising down Redwood Street, dodging senior-citizen drivers, when I swung my leg over his, trying to step on the brake. "Stop for a sec."

"Lacey!" he yelled. "You want to get us killed?"

"No, I want you to pull over and stop."

He did, making a brat face. Sometimes I wished Gel would grow up. I rolled the car window all the way down. "Jessica!" I shouted. "Jessica!"

As she trotted over to the car, Gel leaned forward to take a good look at her in her nylon running shorts and tank top.

"Working out?" I asked her.

She nodded yes and leaned down to look in the car window. Gel unbuckled his seat belt and moved closer to me so she'd notice him. Like there was something to notice.

"Did you pick up a team shirt for me?"

She shook her head. "I asked, but Mrs. Krebs wouldn't let me take it."

"There's your mistake—never ask," I told her. "Stop breathing on me, Gel."

"Krebsy said that if you start coming to practice, she'll make sure you get a shirt," Jessica went on. "I'm running in the meet on Monday. Just five of us were chosen. You would've made it, Lacey, if you'd come to practice more—you're a lot faster than Lana. I'm sure Mrs. Krebs will give you another chance."

I tried not to laugh. Like I wanted to get all hot and sweaty with a bunch of track dorks?

"What time does the team get dismissed?" I asked. Like I didn't know.

"The beginning of last period." Then she broke into a big smile. "Hey, on Monday that's math!"

"How *lucky*," I said. "Listen, maybe we can get together tomorrow."

"Cool!" she replied. "Want to do our workout?"

"Sure. I'll call you in the morning."

She waved to Gel and me and jogged on.

"Does she have a boyfriend?" Gel asked as he pulled away from the curb.

"A guy in ninth grade and a guy in prep school," I told him. "And an E-mail pal at a college in New York City."

"Oh."

I sighed. Sometimes I wished Gel would grow a brain and not believe everything I say.

92

Jessica

The next day—Sunday—when I got home from my workout, everyone else was out and there was a message on the answering machine. "Where are you?" Lacey demanded. "I thought we had plans."

I called her back, slightly annoyed. "We had plans for this *morning,*" I reminded her. "It's now afternoon, two-thirty or so." I hadn't phoned Lacey's house earlier—she kept telling me not to. Besides, I didn't want to look desperate. Waiting around for Lacey seemed to be my new hobby. *It's time to get a life,* I decided.

"Oh, well, Gel came over," she said lazily. "When you didn't hear from me, you should have just gone ahead and run."

"I did."

Lacey was silent for a moment, which made me happy. I wanted her to know that I wasn't just going to sit around waiting for her forever. "So, what are you doing this afternoon?" she asked.

93

"Haven't decided yet."

"You want to go skating? Meet me here," she said, giving me her address before I had a chance to say yes or no. "We'll go to Windy Hill Park." Was this her way of apologizing to me? I guessed it was. You can't expect someone as cool as Lacey to just come out and say they're sorry. Well—I could forgive her this time. At least she was getting the message that she couldn't just stand me up whenever she felt like it.

After hanging up and changing my clothes three times, I finally put on a pair of jeans and a pink shirt, then bladed over to Lacey's house. She answered the door in black Lycra leggings and a guy's shirt that was buttoned halfway up from the bottom. I could see a black sports bra underneath and a silver chain around her neck with a cross dangling from it. She looked maximum cool and three years older than me.

"Come in a sec," she said. "No one's home. I've got to get money."

I removed my skates and entered the front hall. Since Mom is a decorator, I've seen photographs of a lot of strange houses, but this was the weirdest one ever. Everything in it was black or white—everything but one little toy. Penelope's rabbit, the one I had chased and Damon Ross had rescued from the mall fountain, was lying on the sofa, still blue. The rest of the house was like something in an old black-and-white TV show, the kind they run sometimes on cable. Only those houses also had shades of gray.

Lacey looked at me. "I know you're wondering why I don't just wear prison stripes," she said.

"It *is* different," I admitted, then added, "I guess it's only a prison if you don't want to be here."

"I don't. And they don't want me to be either. That's the one thing we agree on."

I watched her take cash from three different places: a purse in an office, which I figured was her stepmother's; a drawer in another office—probably her father's; and a jar in the kitchen. She took just a few dollars from each. *Taking money from her parents is no big deal,* I told myself. *They'll never even notice.* So why did I feel like Lacey was stealing?

"You've brought bucks, right?" she asked. "In case we see something we need. If you didn't, there's another place where they keep money for the baby-sitters."

No way did I want her taking anything for me. "I have enough," I told her.

"Then we're out of here."

It was a relief to be out of that house—like I really had escaped from prison. Lacey and I sat on the front step and put on our skates.

"Which way to the park?" I asked. "I never go to Windy Hill."

She pointed and we started off, skating in sync at first. The roads we took were steep. I was surprised—I could skate uphill faster than I used to. Lacey lagged behind.

"I guess I don't have to do any running for cross-country today," she remarked.

"So you're still interested in it?"

"Sure," she replied. "My life's just not as simple as yours, so I can't always make practice."

"Oh." What did she mean by *simple?* Was that a dis? What did Lacey even know about my life anyway?

"Let's cruise a little," Lacey said as we approached the park's entrance. "Then we'll stop at the bridge. Someone's always hanging out there."

"Sounds good."

We passed between old stone pillars, then skated down a road under high, arching trees. The trees were pretty—like a ceiling in a long church—but there was a lot of trash blowing around. Benches along the road were covered with graffiti. Some patches of grass were mostly mud; other places were full of weeds.

Lacey was a natural on skates and wove in and out of people in the park, performing spins. Old men out for Sunday walks and a group of kids on bikes admired the girl in black zipping by with her chestnut hair tossing in the breeze.

"Stop a minute," I called to Lacey, and we rolled over to a bench. My French braid had come unraveled. I shook it loose and started piling it into a ponytail.

Lacey took a pack of cigarettes from her shirt pocket and held it out to me. "Want one?"

"Not right now," I said, pretending I had to work on a bad knot in my hair.

She stuck the cigarette in her mouth, pulled out a lighter, and puffed for a moment. The cigarette looked long and slim in her fingers. She held it as if she'd been smoking since she was three, casually flicking off ashes, looking ultra-cool. But it smelled bad. It made me think of my dad's friend who smoked. His breath and clothes always stank.

"Ready for one now?" Lacey asked, tossing the pack to me.

"I can't smoke and run," I said, handing it back. "I mean, I can't run at my best."

"Sure, you can," she insisted. "It's not like you're forty years old."

"But I don't *want* to." I wished my voice hadn't sounded so whiny. I had never smoked, and I didn't intend to start now. But I didn't want Lacey to think I was a baby either.

She shrugged and slipped the pack into her pocket. After another long drag she tossed her half-smoked cigarette into the grass and started off. I followed her, wondering what my twin would have thought of that move. I could just see Elizabeth diving after the butt, saving the environment. "Where's the bridge?" I asked.

"You'll see. Around this bend."

We skated up and over the wide span of the bridge, then Lacey made a sharp right, her wheels spinning over gravel. She headed downhill toward a stream, reaching out suddenly for a tree to stop herself. I swung around on the other side of the tree, hoping its skinny trunk was strong enough to keep both of us from tumbling down to the water. We snapped off a few twigs, but we stopped.

The stream ran on a concrete bed that disappeared under the stone bridge. I could hear voices echoing below us.

"I don't usually go down this hill in skates," Lacey said, first trying to walk down it sideways, then finally sitting down to remove her skates.

I did the same, unlacing them and listening to the voices, wondering who was under the bridge. We opened our backpacks. I slipped into a pair of brown clogs, and Lacey tied on some chunky black lace-ups.

"Hey, it's Lacey girl," someone called out as we walked toward the shadowy area under the big arch.

"Hey, Lynx," she replied.

When my eyes got used to the darkness, I saw five people camped on the damp concrete bank.

"Who's with you?"

"A new friend. Jessica."

"Jessy, Jessy, with the messy gold hair, I want to dance with you tonight," a different guy sang. His voice sounded older. I was sure I'd heard it before . . . somewhere. I'd heard the name Lynx too. Then I remembered: Lynx was the lead guitar in the band Splendora! The other guy must be their singer. I could hardly believe it. She had finally introduced me to the band—I guess Lacey didn't think I was a nerd after all.

"Hi," I said, trying not to sound like I was eight years old.

"Hello," the singer said softly. He was really good-looking. Better than Damon Ross, if that's possible.

"Where's Gel?" a girl asked. She had brown hair with wide blond stripes in it and long bare legs that she draped over Lynx's lap.

"Who knows?" Lacey replied, sitting on the cement slope. I dropped down next to her. "Sometimes I get real tired of Gel."

Jessica

I wondered if Splendora was made up of Gel's friends—they were closer to his age than ours.

"That's cool with me. I'd rather look at *her* anyway," said the singer, eyeing me.

I blushed, and he laughed quietly. If I ever showed up at a dance with him, I'd be the coolest kid in the school, the coolest kid in a *high* school.

"Don't take Rocky seriously," said a guy wearing blue mirror sunglasses and sitting off to one side. "We made him lead singer because he was so busy watching girls, he couldn't sing and play an instrument at the same time." I felt a little light-headed. *I can't keep all of these people straight,* I thought.

Rocky just laughed, a deep laugh that gave me goose bumps and made me want to hear it again.

"Lacey, did Gel tell you about the gig Monday?" asked another girl. She had red hair and a snake tattoo that wrapped around her wrist.

Lacey nodded. "The party at Seafront—some rich kid trying to act cool."

"Rich kids pay well," the redhead replied. "If you can stand those baby-sitting gigs."

I didn't know what she meant by that, but I laughed when all the others did.

"Can we count on you as a roadie?" the redhead asked Lacey.

"I'll be there," she replied.

100

I wished they would ask me. I'd love to be one of the people that helps a band set up. Especially if the band is Splendora!

"Seafront's a couple of hours away. We'll be leaving at two," the girl continued, leaning back against the concrete bank and putting her hands behind her head to cushion it. She didn't wear a bra—that was obvious. I saw Rocky eyeing *her* now. If only I had worn a gray tank top or something. In my pink cotton shirt I must have looked like a little girl who had just wandered in from a birthday party.

"I can do two o'clock," Lacey said with confidence. "I can do earlier. I've got an excuse for skipping out last period." She glanced sideways at me.

Lynx smiled. "Yeah? Does Jessica write notes for you and sign your stepmom's name?" He sounded sarcastic.

"It's easier than that when you plan ahead," Lacey answered coolly. I wondered what she meant. I racked my brain for something to say but came up dry. I didn't want Splendora to think I was mute or something.

"I don't get why you don't just skip out altogether," remarked the girl with the striped hair. "I did."

"Yeah, but Lacey likes her daddy's money," Lynx said.

101

Lacey ignored him. "You can count on me to be there to load the van and on Jessica to cover for me."

I looked at her, surprised, then tried to look cool again, like I'd known this all along. Had she been *planning* it all along?

Maybe Lacey read my face and was afraid I'd blurt out something dumb. She jumped up quickly. "Well, we've got to roll. See you tomorrow."

"Bye, Jessy with the messy golden hair," Rocky called. "I'd still like to dance with you."

"Bye," I said, my voice sounding shy.

I didn't want to leave. Lacey pulled me out from under the bridge and pushed me up the slope to the road above. Sitting on the bridge's wall, she tugged on her skates, a fierce expression on her face.

I waited for her mood to get better, then gave up and asked, "Have you been a roadie for them before?"

"Lots." She started down the slope of the bridge like a speed skater.

I took my time fastening my skates. I didn't think she'd disappear without telling me what I was supposed to do on Monday. Just as I had guessed, she was waiting for me where the road curved back toward the park entrance.

"How are you going to skip out of math

102

class?" I asked when I'd caught up with her.

"Leave with the team, how else?" Lacey replied. "Of course, I won't go as far as the locker room." She looked me in the eye. "You'll back me up if a teacher stops me, right?"

I didn't know what to say. If I'd been given the chance, I'd want to travel with the band too. And maybe I'd get a chance if I helped Lacey out this one time. But . . .

"We'll probably get back late," she went on. "All I need is for you to handle a call from my dad. If he phones your house, tell him the team went out to eat together and everybody's doing homework at your house."

I thought about it for a moment. "What if he wants to speak to you?"

"He won't," she replied. She sounded absolutely sure.

"But how do you know that—"

"Just pick up the phone before anybody else," she cut me off. "Then say exactly what I told you. My father will be glad I'm not home to stir up trouble. He'll want to hang up as soon as he can—he doesn't waste time, not when it comes to me. Trust me."

The last two words seemed to jump out at me. *Trust me*. Could I?

"I'm counting on you to be cool about this—Jessy

with the messy golden hair," she added. "So how do you like Rocky?"

"He's cute," I said. I really wanted to see him again. And my only excuse to see him was Lacey.

"You know, if you had gotten me that team shirt, tomorrow's escape would have been a lot easier to pull off," Lacey said.

I didn't answer her, just followed her through the park gates silently. Nothing had been easy since the day I'd started at the junior high. And I was pretty sure tomorrow wasn't going to be any different.

Elizabeth

As soon as I stepped off the school bus on Monday morning, Anna called to me from across the parking lot.

"Hi," I said, feeling kind of uncomfortable. Did Anna still want me to quit the paper? It didn't look like Salvador was going to resign, and I wasn't ready to either. But I wished I had at least mentioned my ecology article to her so she'd know I had tried again. "Anna," I said hesitantly, "listen, I haven't decided yet what I'm going to do about the *Spectator*."

She nodded. "Okay," she said, sounding confident that the only decision I could make was to quit. "Speak of the devil."

Charlie had just climbed out of a large, black car. Seeing us, she walked quickly in our direction, taking long strides in her chunky-heeled shoes. Her regular glasses sat on top of her head, and a pair of sunglasses, whose corners turned upward like wings, rested on her nose.

"Good morning, Elizabeth. Anna."

"Hi." I managed a weak smile.

"Hello, Charlie," Anna said with a slight smirk.

"I have fantastic news for you, Elizabeth," Charlie gushed. "We've accepted your article on the polluted stream."

Anna's eyes widened with surprise.

"We all think it's excellent," Charlie went on.

"You wrote another article?" Anna asked, a look of disbelief on her face. Then her expression changed—she looked like I had just stabbed her in the back.

"The powers that be met Friday night and read it over," Charlie continued. "It's exactly what we had in mind."

"Congratulations," Anna said softly.

I heard the quiver in her voice. I felt awful, like I had betrayed her. But I had never *said* I was going to quit. I had a right to try one more time. And there was nothing wrong with wanting to hang out with Salvador. Was there?

I heard Anna take a deep breath. "I'll see you later, Elizabeth," she said, then turned and headed quickly for the school building.

Charlie glanced after Anna. "Some people aren't willing to work hard and learn," she remarked.

"Maybe, but that's not true about Anna," I pointed out.

"Anyway," Charlie said, "we've accepted your article. And as I said, we think it's excellent—with a few minor changes, of course."

A few minor changes? How about ripping it up and burning it, for starters? I thought. But I didn't say anything—just nodded.

"The editors have been talking over the weekend." Charlie paused and smiled at me as if she were about to announce a wonderful surprise. "We'd like you to be our permanent environmental reporter. How does that sound?"

"Uh, well . . ." I tried to imagine myself turning out a series of depressing pieces on all the things people were doing to ruin the world. I imagined seeing my name as the byline of boring, boring articles, news stories that only a copy editor and my mother would read. Was there any way hanging out with Salvador could make up for that?

"Think about it," Charlie said as we started walking toward the school. "We believe you have a real talent for it. In the meantime your article on the stream will be coming out in the next issue."

And then someone might read it—gag. "About that article," I said. "Would it be all right if I used a pen name?"

She stopped and turned to me, her eyebrows rising above her sunglasses. "A pseudonym? Why would you want to write under a fictitious name?"

"Well," I said, searching for a reason—other than the fact that I was ashamed of the piece. "Well, I thought it might be fun. I could sign the article something like . . . uh . . . Ima Frogg or Frieda Whales."

She cocked her head.

"You know, free-the-whales, *Free Willie*," I rattled on. Okay, so my puns were worse than my father's.

"Why would you want to do that?" she asked again.

I stood on the edge of the yellow curb and wrapped my arms tightly around my schoolbooks. Why would I allow her to publish the awful thing at all? Why would I allow myself to be publicly humiliated, that was the real question. *I should have quit with Anna*, I thought. *I should have quit, I should have quit.* "You're right," I agreed. "I don't want to use a pen name. I want to withdraw the article."

"Excuse me?"

"I'd like to withdraw my article," I said. "I don't think it's good enough to be published."

"I believe that's my decision, not yours," Charlie snapped.

"Still," I replied softly, "it's my article, and I'm withdrawing it."

"Writers often have inferiority complexes,"

she said in a more soothing voice. "That's why they need editors like me, to give them guidance and confidence."

"Charlie, I'm really sorry, but what I'm saying is that you can't publish it, okay?"

She stared at me. "Think about what you're doing, Elizabeth," she warned. "The editors and I won't be interested in reading and working as hard as we do to whip your articles into shape if you withdraw them afterward. Our time is valuable."

"I understand," I assured her. "I'll pick up my article from the journalism room later today."

"Fine," she said. "Have it your way." She turned on her heels and strode inside the school doors.

A wave of relief washed over me. I still wasn't totally ready to resign. Right now, I just wanted to get my article back and find Anna to straighten things out with her.

I started toward the school's glass doors, then heard quick footsteps coming up behind me.

"Elizabeth!"

"Hey, Salvador," I said. "I can't believe you're here already, I mean, actually on time! Is everything all right?"

"I saw you talking to Charlie," he said, looking uncomfortable. "Listen, Elizabeth, there's something I have to tell you before you find out from someone else. I was rejected," he blurted out.

Elizabeth

I stared at him for a moment, not understanding what he meant. "Rejected—by a girl?" As soon as I said it, I wanted to crawl in a hole and die.

He smiled a little, then the smile disappeared. "By the newspaper. I found out Friday morning, but I couldn't tell you. I was afraid that—I dunno. Anyway, Anna said it was no big deal and I should tell you, but . . ."

He glanced away. Until then I hadn't realized that Salvador's self-confidence could be beaten back. But the slope of his shoulders told me he had taken his rejection to heart.

"I'm sorry they didn't take your work," I said. "And Anna's right—it really is no big deal."

He didn't meet my eyes.

"Salvador, I was looking at the cartoons they published in their back issues. You've seen them. Would you want people to think you did them?

"*I* wouldn't," I said when he didn't reply. "Listen, it's not your problem if the staff doesn't know good stuff when they see it. It's not your problem that Mr. Lime should be working in a museum and doesn't understand—"

I broke off. He looked miserable—maybe I was saying all the wrong things. I shut my mouth and hugged him.

I'm not sure who was more surprised by that—him or me. I kept my head down, afraid to look up at his face. His shirt felt soft against my cheek. He rested one hand on my back very gently. I quickly let go. "I just want you to feel better," I said, backing away.

His dark eyes shone. "I do. Um, if I submit more cartoons, maybe one a day, do I get a hug for each rejection?"

I could feel my cheeks getting warm. "So anyway," I said.

"So anyway," he repeated, "have you submitted anything else to the *Spectator*?"

"Yes, an article on the polluted stream, but I withdrew it."

"Why?" he asked.

"It was awful. I rewrote it four or five times. Each time it was terrible in a new way."

Salvador laughed. "Then Charlie will want it."

I was silent for a moment. I didn't want to make Salvador feel worse, but I didn't want to lie to him either. That's how feelings get hurt. I had just learned my lesson with Anna: It's best to be straight with friends.

"She does. The editors have accepted it, and Charlie's pretty annoyed that I've withdrawn it. And I think Anna's mad."

Salvador looked at me for a long moment, then touched my cheek with one finger. Suddenly he threw back his head and laughed.

Elizabeth

"You got accepted, but you look more miserable than me, who got rejected." He gave me a hug.

I felt the softness of his shirt again and the warmth of his arms loose around my back.

"I just want you to feel better," he whispered.

I did.

Jessica

I'd spent Sunday night daydreaming, imagining myself winning the meet, then joining Rocky at his concert afterward. With major things like that on my mind, it was pretty easy to forget the history assignment due Monday. Which was why I was stuck in the library at lunchtime.

Well, it was one place Lacey wouldn't look for me. I didn't want to talk to her about her plans to escape this afternoon. I didn't feel real good about covering for her, but I didn't want to let her down either. How could we be friends if I didn't back her up? What if she told Rocky I was a goody-goody who wouldn't help out a friend?

I sighed and closed a book about the gold rush. "In conclusion," I wrote, though I hadn't come to any. I scribbled a final sentence on my report, picked up my books, and headed to my locker to grab lunch. If I got lucky, my weird locker partner, Ronald, would still be in the cafeteria or in his favorite place, the math center.

No such luck. Ronald was kneeling in front of our locker, staring at the metal door, deep in thought. Still trying to discover the world's biggest prime number, I figured—it was his goal in life. But I didn't say anything. The last thing you wanted to do with Ronald was get him into a conversation.

I tiptoed up to the locker and pretended to be invisible as I piled things into it.

"You've got mail," he announced, sounding like the computerized voice on our family's E-mail account.

I glanced down. It was my mail he was staring at, stuffed through the vents in the door and stuck there.

I quickly knelt to get it. "You don't read my notes, do you?" I asked.

"Only what I can see when I hold them up to the light," he replied. "There's another note here that someone dropped on top of my books."

I snatched up both messages and quickly unfolded the first:

Jessica,
     Where are you? Couldn't find you in the caf, and Kristin said she hadn't seen you.

I got a team shirt. The equipment room was locked, but I had my ID card and it always works on those kinds of locks.

I think even Principal Plugnose is helping me out today, wishing the team good luck in the morning announcements. Hope Wilfred heard it. See you in math.

Lacey

P.S. Saw Rocky at the gas station last night. Says he still wants to dance with you.

I smiled and felt like I was floating on air. Rocky remembered me! He had sent a message to me—sort of. I couldn't stop smiling.

"Good news?" Ronald asked, breaking the spell. "Good news, Jessica?"

"Yeah, I just got a scholarship from the University of California."

"You did?" he gasped. "For summer studies?"

"Ronald, get real."

I opened the second note.

Jessica,
    Good luck today.
    Run fast as a rabbit
    but stay dry.

The note wasn't signed. I read it again. Run fast as a rabbit but stay dry. What was this—a riddle?

"Um, Ronald?" I began, my voice a little nicer than before. "Did you see who left this note?"

"No," he said, piling books into his bag. "I heard, but I didn't see the person."

I frowned at him. "How is that possible?"

"I was thinking," he replied.

"So what—you can't hear, see, and think at the same time?"

"Not when I have my eyes closed."

Unbelievable.

"Somebody leaned over me to drop it in the locker," he explained.

I rocked back on my heels. "And you still didn't open your eyes! What if it had been a thief, Ronald? What if the person was"—I tried to think of the worst thing that could happen to him—"stealing your math notebook?"

"I would have noticed. I had it in my hand."

"Look," I said, pushing the square piece of paper in front of his face. "This person didn't sign the note. Do you have any clue who might have left it?"

"Their shoes hardly made a noise," he answered. "And the person didn't smell in any particular way."

I shook my head. "Don't plan on being a

detective, Ronald." I scooped up my books, grabbed my Walkman and a couple of tapes off the top shelf, and walked away.

I adjusted the earphones on my head and looked down at the tapes in my hand. The top one was this crazy dance music Steven had bought on a whim and hated. I loved it, so Steven let me have it. The group was called Shonen Knife—they were a Japanese all-girl band. It was great to run to. I wasn't sure I was in the mood for it now, though, so I flipped it over to see what else I had with me.

Shonen Knife again.

I stopped in my tracks and stared at the tapes in disbelief.

What was I doing with two copies of the same tape? Weird.

What was this? Mystery Day?

Maybe someone else had a copy of the tape and I picked it up by mistake, I reasoned. That made sense—if I saw a copy of the tape lying around, I would definitely take it, assuming it was mine. After all, who else would listen to random all-girl Japanese dance music?

That was the question. Who else?

I gave up and shoved both tapes and my Walkman in my backpack. This mystery would have to wait—I had other puzzles to solve first.

Jessica

As I made my way through the rush of students leaving the cafeteria, I repeated the message to myself. Stay dry. The writer could be Bethel or one of the girls on the team teasing me about my wet shoes. But I didn't think any of them knew where my locker was. Maybe Elizabeth had left the note to cheer me on. No—it didn't look like her handwriting, and Elizabeth wouldn't have disguised it.

Something about the words in the note stuck in my mind. Rabbit. Dry. Rabbit . . . dry. The only rabbit I knew was Penelope's . . . which hadn't stayed dry. *Yes!*

I stared down at the note. Was it possible? Damon Ross might have fished out the rabbit and rescued me from some jerks, but he wouldn't have left this message—would he? He hardly said a word to anyone and did a disappearing act every day after school. Elizabeth had told me he was on the *Spectator* but had missed most of the meetings. No one seemed to know anything about him—except that he acted like he didn't want to be known.

It was probably silly to hope the message was from him. Still, I scratched a quick note, wrapped the unsigned message inside mine, and stuffed the whole thing in Elizabeth's locker. I could count on my twin to be a better detective than Ronald.

A n n a

When I saw her out of the corner of my eye, I quickly ducked behind a tall metal shelf, then peeked between a narrow opening in the books. I thought Elizabeth had worn a green headband today, and she had a white one, but I couldn't believe it was Jessica working in the library. I widened the gap between the books. The blond twin suddenly stood up and gathered her belongings. Purple binder, purple pencil case—Jessica.

So far today I had been able to avoid Salvador, but it had been much harder with Elizabeth, who was in all of my classes. Before and after each class I'd asked my teachers a zillion questions, waving Elizabeth on, telling her I'd catch up with her. Sooner or later I'd have to talk to her and Salvador, but I couldn't yet, not after this morning.

"Hi, Anna!"

I jumped back from my peephole.

Anna

Brian Rainey, who's about a foot taller than I am, scrunched down to look through the space between the books. "Who are you looking at?"

"No one. Just looking," I said.

"That's what my sister says—just looking—like she's shopping in a store. Usually she's shopping for a guy."

"Well, I'm not shopping at all," I told him, but I smiled.

It's hard not to smile around Brian since he's always grinning. He's Salvador's friend and Elizabeth's locker mate, but it was better that he, rather than someone else, had caught me acting stupid. He never made fun of anyone. Maybe being the middle one of five kids, he'd already seen all the dumb things that people can do.

"Salvador's been looking for you, Anna," Brian said.

"Really?" I said, playing dumb. "I haven't seen him." *I'm surprised Salvador has a spare brain cell left to concentrate on me,* I thought. *Let him use them all to think about Elizabeth.*

Brian leaned against the bookshelf, propping one elbow on the edge, studying me. His smile and his eyes, which were a light golden green, as if sunlight were shining in them, always made you feel comfortable talking to him. Not that I'm the kind to tell people secret things like feelings.

Salvador was the only one I ever confided in—
and now not even him.

As if Brian read my mind, he said, "He's worried about you. He says you're keeping things
to yourself."

"Like he's not?" I shot back.

Brian let my anger run off him and continued
on in an easy voice. "I asked Salvador, 'You
mean Anna's not telling you things the way girls
don't tell you things, and then you have to
guess what's bothering them, and half the time
you guess wrong?'"

"What did he say to that?" I asked curiously.

"'That's girls. I'm talking about Anna.'"

I gave a disgusted grunt. "*That* figures."

"So I reminded him that you are one," Brian said.

I didn't know whether to thank him or cry.

"Gee, I can tell I made you feel better," he observed, one side of his mouth drawing up in a
lopsided grin. "I'm sorry, Anna. I was just trying
to let you know where Salvador's coming from."

"No problem. I already knew. I mean, I'm
Salvador's friend, not his *girl*friend," I said, trying
to keep the bitterness out of my voice. "He already has that covered," I added under my breath.

Brian was quiet for a moment. "Maybe I
shouldn't ask this. But do you have, uh, different
feelings for him than you used to?"

"I don't want to be Salvador's girlfriend, if that's what you mean. Absolutely, positively not."

"But you don't want anybody else to be either," he guessed.

I looked at him, surprised. "Yeah. That's it exactly." Anybody else—like Elizabeth. "That's really selfish of me, isn't it?"

"More like normal, I think," Brian said. Then he suddenly craned his neck and peered around the end of the library shelf. "Ms. Dewey," he whispered, dropping down in a crouch, pulling me with him. "I don't think she's made her quota for detention slips this month."

We waited till the librarian had passed, then sat down on the floor across from each other, leaning back against opposite shelves.

"You know," Brian said, "when I was a kid, I wanted my brother Billy to disappear. I'd have done anything to have a different bedroom from him—a different CD system, a different name. If kidnappers had shown up at our house, I'd have paid them to take him. Then Billy got a girlfriend. Then he invited his girlfriend to go to the lake with us, the one where we always fish. I liked Jenny—she was supernice. But when Billy invited her out in our rowboat, I wanted *her* to disappear. Know what I mean?"

I nodded. "So what did you do?"

"Threw her overboard."

I laughed out loud.

"Shhh."

"Brian, do you think you can be as close to someone—I mean, as close as you were before when that person gets a boyfriend or girlfriend?"

He ran his hand through his blond hair. "In my wide experience—meaning my brother and my sister—not if they're doing the falling-in-love stuff."

"I hate it when people change," I said bitterly. "I just hate it!"

Brian stayed quiet.

"It's unfair," I cried, "when someone changes on you—when you're the same but they're not."

"You can't stop people from changing, Anna," he said softly.

"Well, you can stop hanging around them and trusting them with things that matter to you. You can stop making yourself feel lousy by watching them change." I shrugged and looked him in the eye. "I don't really care anyway."

Brian didn't blink. "It's a rough time for you," he said.

When I didn't reply, Brian stood up. Reaching down, he took my hands in his and gently pulled me to my feet. He could have taught Salvador a thing or two about how to treat a friend . . . and a girl.

Salvador

"Jessica!" I called out to Elizabeth's sister.

To me, she'll always be *Elizabeth's sister*. I was starting to think of math class as "the class Elizabeth is in" and bus number 402 as "Elizabeth's bus," like she was the only one who rode it. Which maybe should worry me.

"El Salvador," Jessica replied, turning around just before she entered the classroom.

Inside the room Mr. Wilfred was sitting at his desk, marking papers and punching numbers on his calculator.

"You sure do know how to manage things," I told Jessica. "How did you get Mrs. Krebs to schedule an away meet on the day you had math last period?"

Jessica's eyes widened. "I didn't do any such thing!"

I took a step back. Did you ever feel like, with some people, no matter what you said, it was going to be the wrong thing?

"It was a joke," I said. "But then, you never get my jokes."

At that, she smiled.

"I have info about your mysterious note," I told her.

"Yeah?"

"When Elizabeth and I stopped by the journalism room to pick up our submissions, we poked around. The good news is that it could be Damon's handwriting. The bad news is it could also be Ted or Charlie's. They all have that funny backward slant. Should we submit the note to the FBI for analysis?"

"No, it was just a hunch," she said. "It's not like it matters to me," she added with a casual wave of her hand.

"Well, since it's no big deal, I'll just go ahead and ask Damon about it."

"Don't you dare!" she exclaimed.

I laughed and started down the hall. "Hey, Jessica," I said, turning around. "I meant to tell you—break a leg!"

Jessica

"That's a theater expression," Bethel said as she entered the math room behind me. "Break a leg means good luck. You psyched?"

"Yeah. A little nervous too." I wouldn't have admitted that to Bethel a week ago, but she was smiling. And I was starting to think I could be straight with her. Bethel didn't set out to dis people. She only did that when they had already dissed her or someone else.

"Don't worry. Nervous is good," she told me. "If you're too sure of yourself, you won't run well. I should know," Bethel added, grinning. "I was real confident in a race last summer and got run over. Left behind like roadkill."

"I don't believe it," I said, laughing at the way she'd put it.

"Trust me," she replied.

Those words echoed in my ears. Lacey had told me the same thing. How strange that those two would use the same expression—they

126

seemed so different. But were they? I looked at Bethel more closely. What did I really know about Bethel—or Lacey, for that matter? I knew that neither one of them cared what anyone thought of them. I knew that they could both be rude. But the difference was that Bethel had *stopped* being rude to me. Could I say the same about Lacey, the girl I called a friend?

In some ways, I realized, *I know more about Bethel than I do about Lacey.* For example, I knew that Bethel always put her left shoe on first. And I knew that she always left her things behind in the locker room. . . . Suddenly something occurred to me. I opened my backpack. "Is this yours?" I asked, holding up the Shonen Knife tape.

Her eyes opened wide. "Where did you find it?"

"In the locker room, I guess," I replied. "I must have thought it was mine. I have the same tape."

She looked at me when I said that, and we stood there a moment, staring at each other.

"That's funny," Bethel said softly.

"Girls, you're blocking the door," Mr. Wilfred called from his desk. We started toward our seats.

"Hey, teammates!" Lacey called from the door of the classroom. Both Bethel and I turned around.

Lacey was wearing a purple team shirt, running shorts, and athletic shoes. She had put her hair in a French braid just like mine.

Jessica

I heard Bethel let out her breath in a disgusted way. Not that I blamed her. I was kind of annoyed that Lacey was going to use track as an excuse to leave school when she had ditched practice—and me—so many times. Oh, well. I was too far in to back out now.

"Are you all ready for our meet?" Lacey asked as she walked toward us.

When Bethel didn't reply, I said, "Yeah. Yeah, we are."

"Me too," Lacey told us, then gave a big laugh.

Bethel walked to her seat without saying a word.

"Did you get my note?" Lacey asked me.

I nodded and glanced sideways at Mr. Wilfred, wondering just how good his hearing was. He was concentrating on the papers in front of him, holding his red pen like a weapon, marking them furiously.

"Pretty cool, huh?" she went on. "I mean, don't take this the wrong way, Jessica, but I never guessed Rocky would be sending *you* a message."

At the thought of Rocky, my impatience with Lacey faded. I thought of the soft, low way Rocky laughed. I thought of what his voice sounded like singing, "Jessy, Jessy, with the messy golden hair." I got goose bumps all over.

"Maybe he'll dedicate a song to you at the gig tonight. I'll let you know tomorrow, okay?"

She strolled to her seat.

Dedicate a song to me? I imagined Splendora playing at the Manchester, our local teen club. Elizabeth would be there with Salvador. And Brian and some other cool kids. I'd call up friends from my old school and say, "I haven't seen you for so long, I have free tickets, stop by the club, okay?" Lacey and I would hang out by the stage because we had helped the band set up. I imagined everyone's face when Rocky sang a song he had written for me, "Jessy with the Messy Golden Hair."

"Miss Wakefield? Miss Wakefield!" Mr. Wilfred's voice cut into my dream.

Everybody in the class had sat down. I hurried to my desk at the back of the room.

We opened our books to the problems on page eighteen, and Mr. Wilfred began his heavy bee drone. I could have used him last night when I was too excited to sleep. Like then, my mind was spinning.

Would the course at the meet have steeper hills than the ones we ran at practice? Would every runner be as fast as Bethel? Would Mr. Wilfred question us when we got up to leave for the meet? If I didn't cover for Lacey, would I get a chance to know Rocky? I knew the answer to that last question: No way.

Jessica

So what? I could cover for her easily. Covering for somebody was a whole lot different from actually making up a lie. It wasn't like I was fooling my family or friends—just Mr. Wilfred and Lacey's father—and I didn't care about them. That kind of lie didn't count.

So why was I so worried about it?

"Miss Wakefield, the answer, please?"

"Um . . . I'm not sure."

"Perhaps if you listened," Mr. Wilfred said, "you would be."

Lacey, who was sitting two seats in front of me, put her hand casually over her shoulder, then wiggled her fingers at me. She could make her fingers do funny things, like she was double-jointed. The girl between Lacey and me hunched over, her shoulders shaking. I quickly looked down at my book to keep from laughing out loud.

We moved on to page nineteen. The book had 320 pages. It was going to be a very long year.

Suddenly three bells chimed, the signal that an announcement was about to be made over the PA system. I saw Lacey straighten up in front of me. Two aisles over, Bethel shifted in her chair, then reached to pull her schoolbooks out of the rack beneath her desk.

"Pardon this interruption," the principal said, his nose sounding plugged up as usual.

"The girls from the cross-country team are now dismissed to the locker room. Good luck, girls. Bring home a win for Sweet Valley Junior High!"

I rose from my seat the same time as Bethel. Lacey didn't. I guess I'd been holding my breath because I let out a long sigh of relief.

Then Lacey stood up.

I saw Bethel's head jerk over in our direction. But Mr. Wilfred, who was busy writing on the board, didn't notice. "Make sure you get your homework assignment from one of your fellow students," he told us, without even glancing at us. What a break!

I followed Lacey down the aisle.

Bethel stood still. "Where are you going, Lacey?" she asked.

Oh no. Why couldn't Bethel be even a *little* intimidated by Lacey? It would have made my life so much easier. Mr. Wilfred turned around. He hated any kind of speaking out in class.

"To the meet," Lacey answered in a low, clear voice. "Weren't you there when Mrs. Krebs said the entire team is supposed to go?"

"I was there when she said you hadn't earned a place on the team," Bethel replied coolly.

Mr. Wilfred looked from one girl to the other, frowning. I figured he was more annoyed that his class was being interrupted than concerned that Lacey might be skipping out.

"Sorry, Bethel," Lacey said, "you heard wrong. She gave me a team shirt."

Bethel shook her head, then glanced at me, as if to ask how Lacey had gotten a shirt.

I could cover for Lacey—I could shrug off people like Mr. Wilfred, who was probably just as glad to get Lacey out of his classroom. But I didn't want to lie to Bethel. Maybe she wasn't a good friend of mine, but I respected her. Somehow I knew she wouldn't lie to *me*. I looked away.

"Girls, we're waiting to get on with our lesson," Mr. Wilfred said. "Are you staying or going?"

I guessed the team shirt convinced him.

"Come on, Jessica," Lacey said. As soon as Wilfred turned to write on the board, she gave me a look like, "Why are you screwing this up?"

Something occurred to me suddenly. Maybe Lacey joined the team just to get out of class. Would she ask me to cover for her every time the team had a meet? I had a bad feeling that eventually there would be other lies she'd want me to tell. "Trust me," she'd said when we were skating yesterday. But why should I? Had she ever acted like a real friend to me?

"Hurry up," Lacey said impatiently. "You haven't even changed into your uniform yet."

"None of the *team* has," Bethel observed, still standing by her desk.

"What's your problem, Bethel?" Lacey hissed.

"My problem is that you aren't on the team!" Bethel replied.

Mr. Wilfred glanced at me. "Miss Wakefield," he said. "I don't usually look to you for answers, but could you tell me whether Miss Frells is on the team?"

"Tell him, Jessica," Lacey encouraged me. When I hesitated, Lacey turned to Mr. Wilfred. "Bethel doesn't like me," she said. "Since the first day of practice she has done anything she can to make things tough for me."

Wait a minute, I thought. There was only one day when Bethel had made it tough for Lacey—the same day Lacey had made it tough for Jan.

"She lies about me to the coach," Lacey continued.

What?

"Isn't that true, Jessica?" she demanded, glaring at me.

I looked her in the eye. What could I do? Lacey was forcing me to choose. "No, it isn't," I said.

Bethel stared at me with surprise. Mr. Wilfred rubbed his forehead. He was getting his these-kids-are-giving-me-a-migraine look. I knew he just wanted us to leave, but I wasn't about to go before he knew the truth.

"Lacey is dead wrong about Bethel," I told him. "She's a real team person and encourages everyone to do her best. And Bethel doesn't lie."

Bethel's face grew softer, though she didn't actually smile at me. Lacey's eyes blazed, but all of a sudden I didn't care. It was one thing for her to mess with me—to blow me off whenever she felt like it and then expect me to cover for her. But I wasn't about to let her mess with Bethel.

"Lacey has missed too many practices to be on the team," I finished.

"Liar!" Lacey cried. "Why are you saying this stuff, Jessica?"

"Because it's true." *And maybe because Bethel's opinion matters more to me than yours.* Teammates—and friends—have to be able to trust each other.

"You may sit down, Miss Frells," Mr. Wilfred said to Lacey. "We'll have a little chat after school."

So much for Rocky, I thought dismally.

Bethel and I left the classroom quietly.

"You keep surprising me," she said as we headed toward the locker room.

I had to smile at that. "I feel the same way about you."

Anna

Thirty seconds after the final bell of the school day, kids were rushing in all directions.

"Anna! Stop!" Salvador called down to me from the second floor.

At the exact same time the softer voice of Elizabeth called from below the steps where I was standing, "Anna, wait! I've been trying to talk to you all day."

I was caught on the landing between the first and second floor, with no way to escape.

"Why have you been hiding?" Salvador asked me bluntly.

"Why have you been looking in the wrong places?" I replied.

We stared at each other for a moment, then Elizabeth interjected, "Anna, did you read the note I left on your desk in English class?"

I shook my head and searched my pockets for the folded piece of paper.

"We were wondering if you wanted to go to Vito's tonight at about five-thirty," Elizabeth said.

"I'm treating," Salvador added.

"If I can get a ride from Steven, I'll pick you up on the way," Elizabeth volunteered.

"Sorry. I can't make it," I said rather coldly.

Elizabeth looked disappointed—and kind of hurt.

Who cared? Did I have to be nice to someone who stole my best friend? Or to the friend who was willing to be stolen? If her feelings were hurt, let her write an article about it for the *Spectator*. I was sure Salvador would volunteer to help.

"Why not?" Salvador asked.

I thought quickly. "I have to help my mother . . . with some cleaning."

It sounded like the feeble excuse it was. Salvador looked annoyed.

Well, so am I! I thought. *Salvador can't expect me to be there every time he decides he wants me around.* I wasn't his younger sister, waiting for him to pay attention to me. I wasn't his little buddy, hoping he'd invite me along with his "special" friend.

"I've got to run," I said, feeling tears rising in my eyes, knowing I'd die if I had to explain how I felt. I flew down the steps to the nearest exit out of the school.

I tried not to care that they didn't run after me.

Jessica

"Hey, everybody, c'mere," Bethel called as we stood on a field behind Vineyard Pass School, struggling to safety pin paper numbers to our jerseys. The judges at the finish line use those numbers to record the order in which the runners cross it. In cross-country meets the officials add up the places in which your team-mates finish. If you come in first, second, third, fourth, and fifth, your team score is the total of that: fifteen. The team with the lowest total score wins. "Mrs. Krebs, over here," Bethel shouted again.

"Did you find them?" our coach asked her.

Bethel nodded, then told the rest of us, "See the girls in the orange shirts—they won the county championship last year. I saw them do it. Check out numbers twenty-five and twenty-seven. They're the fastest of the group, the ones to keep an eye on. But the others aren't exactly turtles."

Jessica

"Wow, look at their trainers!" I said. Everyone on the orange-shirt team wore the same orange-and-black pair.

Bethel laughed. "You have a thing about shoes, don't you?"

"They're racing flats," Krebsy told me. "They don't hold up like trainers because they're extra light, but when you race in them, you fly."

Great—I was going to run with the flying former county champs. Racing against the five top runners from each school was a whole lot different from running with slower girls from my own school, I realized. I watched numbers twenty-five and twenty-seven. You could see their confidence in the way they walked and in the way they surveyed the rest of us. Especially twenty-five, who had legs like Michael Jordan.

"They're kind of cocky, if you ask me," Bethel remarked. "I wouldn't mind seeing number twenty-five bite the dust."

"Me neither," I said. We grinned at each other.

Mrs. Krebs called us into a huddle then and told us to do our "personal best."

"Let's show 'em, SVJH!" Jan shouted.

"SVJH! SVJH!" we chanted.

A megaphone voice called runners to the starting line. There was some jostling around as thirty girls lined up. The students from each school stuck together.

"Runners, take your mark," the megaphone voice told us. Mary, me, Bethel, Ginger, and Lana each took a step forward, putting our right feet just behind the long starting line, our left feet farther back.

I glanced sideways at Bethel. "Nervous is good, right?"

"Right."

"Get set on the whistle," the voice said.

Bending my knees slightly, I leaned forward from my waist. I felt like I had springs in the back of my legs, tight springs ready to uncoil and send me leaping forward.

I saw the starter raise his gun in the air. I quickly fixed my eyes on the entrance to the woods, about two hundred yards away. The whistle blew. A second later, *bang!*

We were off. Everyone was running hard, running and bunching together at the center. All I could hear were pounding feet and breathing. All I could see was a horizon of bobbing heads. Now I knew how cattle felt in a stampede.

I tried to move ahead. I had to get to the front of the pack—position was everything. But squeezing through was impossible. We were like a monster with a million arms and legs all tangled

Jessica

together. Then someone jammed her elbow hard into my ribs. "Ow! Hey!"

A girl in an orange shirt—number twenty-five—laughed at me and shot by.

"Keep cool," said a quiet voice next to me. Bethel.

Keep cool, I repeated to myself, but I longed for the chance to run over that girl. I watched as she used her elbows to get farther and farther ahead.

"SVJH, we're getting boxed out," Bethel warned.

I glanced around. Mary was on my left. Ginger behind us. Lana trailing.

"Move to the outside. We've got time," Bethel said.

The five of us shifted to the right. It felt good to stretch out my legs, to have my arms suddenly free. Mary took the lead, and the rest of us followed in a wedge shape, steadily passing runners, working our way forward on the outside—forward and gradually back to the middle. We had to get front and center before we reached the woods, where the path was too narrow to pass people easily.

We were closing in on the woods. *We're not going to make it,* I thought. *We're too far behind.* The girls in the orange shirts were up front, with a school in green on their heels. The green shirts were running in a formation that kept other runners from passing them. There was no way we could get around.

"Mary, you take Ginger and Lana to the left. Jess, stick with me," Bethel said, then dropped back, slowing down. It seemed like the wrong thing to do, but I followed her like a shadow. She suddenly dove through to the right. "Now, Jess!"

The girls in green were caught by surprise and shifted quickly, trying to protect both the right and left sides. They left a gap in the middle. We reversed directions. Our legs and arms pumped, and we pushed our way through the center hole. Mary joined us. Now the three of us ran just behind the orange shirts. *Ha, ha!* I thought. *Watch out, twenty-five, I'm gonna getcha!*

We entered the woods. Leaves and sticks crunched and rolled under our feet. The path snaked left and right. Branches whipped at our arms. We leaped over a trickle of a stream.

"Come on, Bethel! Come on, Mary! Do it, Jess!" our teammates hollered to us from behind tree trunks.

"Sharp turn ahead!" Bonnie called.

I heard them cheering Ginger and Lana and figured our running mates weren't too far behind.

We took the turn, leaning into it, ran another hundred yards, and took another sharp turn. Suddenly the woods opened up. The wide sky and field ahead were so bright, I blinked.

"Ugh!" Bethel grunted as we crossed the line from shade to sunlight. The wind blasted in our faces.

We caught up with the orange shirts, and we ran neck and neck in the open field. Slowly they passed us. I wanted to beat them so badly— especially that cocky number twenty-five. I started to pour on the speed, hoping to make her eat my dust. Bethel hissed at me, and Mary reached out and grabbed my shirt.

"What?" I whispered, then slowed down.

"Save it," Bethel said.

"Windbreak," Mary explained.

As soon as I fell in line with my teammates, I felt the difference. The team ahead of us acted like a shield. Though we ran the same pace as they, they had to work much harder to cut through the wind. We let them use up the energy they'd need later on.

"We'll get 'em on the hill," Bethel said.

"You're crazy," I told her.

"I've seen them," Bethel said. "They're weak on hills." She looked at me sideways. "And you're good at them."

I am? I wanted to ask. But I could feel my legs tiring. And the hill ahead of us looked as if it had risen like baked bread. It seemed twice its height since we'd walked the course.

"Come on, SVJH!"

"Short-stride uphill."

"Use your arms!" our teammate-coaches called.

We started up the hill, springing forward on our toes, pumping our arms extra hard. We passed two orange shirts. But twenty-five and twenty-seven were still leading the way and actually picking up speed.

Yeah, sure, they're weak on hills, I thought.

Then we crested the hill. Mary stretched out her long legs and led the charge downward. Suddenly the three of us were a yard past twenty-five and twenty-seven. They had pushed too hard on the uphill and had burned out. Down, down, down we rushed. My eyes blurred with the wind. I hoped my feet would stay under me.

We hit the flat. The final flat, I realized with a jolt. In the distance I saw the finish line. People were jumping up and down, screaming. The orange shirts were right behind us.

"Break!" shouted Bethel, and the three of us blasted off, each running our fastest, each going for it all.

I was running on empty. My lungs felt like they were going to burst. My stomach hurt from sucking down air. But my legs kept going and going, like those of a crazy windup toy. For a moment I was leading the group. Leading!

Then the toe of my shoe caught on something. For a split second I couldn't figure out why I wasn't running anymore. I was on the ground. My knees stung. The palms of my hands burned. My eyes were hot with tears.

A pile of runners was bearing down on me. A dark hand reached down and dragged me up behind her.

Bethel didn't look back, and in a moment she was too far ahead to hear my thank-you.

"Go!" I heard Krebsy holler from the sidelines. "Go!"

I staggered, then started running again. I was going to catch number twenty-five if it killed me—and it just might. I passed one girl, then another and another. I was catching up!

Mary was just in front of me, then she was next to me, then running behind my left shoulder. I kept going. Bethel, twenty-five, and twenty-seven were the only ones in front of me.

Kids screamed and hollered. "SVJH! SVJH!" The chant rang in my ears. Bethel and me and the two orange shirts gunned for the finish line. I passed twenty-seven, but it was number twenty-five I wanted. I was gaining on her, gaining on her, a half step more and I—

Over! I could hardly believe it. Bethel had

snapped the tape and went flying with it down the chute. Number twenty-five went in after her, with me on her heels—third place. Mary crossed the line behind me and then twenty-seven.

Third place, I thought dismally. *I blew it.*

Bethel swung around to Mary and me. "Great run, teammates!"

Third place, I thought.

"We won it. I'm sure," Bethel said, and Mary nodded, a big smile spreading across her face.

Ginger was in the chute—she had come in seventh. Krebsy and the others were cheering Lana down the stretch. There was still a bunch of runners behind her.

My throat was sore, and my legs felt rubbery. Third place.

But I'd done my best. That was all I could do. And it looked like our team had won. What a victory—our brand-new team beating the county champions! I felt light-headed from the win—and from the exertion.

"Put it here," Bethel told me, holding up her hand in a high five.

"I'd like to," I said, "but I think I'm going to barf."

"Friends and Brothers"
by Anna Wang

I lost my wallet once.
Over and over, I looked in my purse,
Under my bed, on my desk—
Even in the refrigerator.
Gone. What a bizarre feeling,
When something you counted on
Isn't there anymore.

This applies to anything.
Like people.
Like—
You.

Elizabeth

"This seat taken?"

"Anna!" I said, surprised and relieved. I slid over in the booth.

"All done with your *cleaning?*" Salvador asked, his voice dripping with sarcasm. Neither of us had believed her excuse for not meeting us at Vito's. I had been worried, but I could tell from Salvador's tone that he was more angry than anything else.

"Didn't do any," Anna replied cheerfully, and sat down on the cracked vinyl seat. "Did you order some pepperoni?"

"Yes," Salvador told her. "I was planning to arrange the little circles in the shape of your face so we'd feel like you were with us. But now we'll just have to eat it."

Both Anna and I laughed.

"Seriously, did you?" she asked. "You know I have to have pepperoni."

"Seriously, I did," he replied. "You *know* I was hoping you'd come."

"Yeah?" Something in her voice told me that she wasn't joking. She wanted a real answer.

"Anna, have you had brain surgery lately?" Salvador asked her.

"Of course I did!"

"I was getting ready to call you from the phone booth," I told her. This was the truth. Because—although I knew I had a right to stay on the paper if I wanted to—I knew Anna had thought I would quit with her. And I felt guilty.

Staying friends with her was way more important to me than the *Spec*.

Anna smiled, and her shoulders relaxed. Things could get complicated when three people became close friends. Had knowing that Salvador and I were still on the paper together made her feel left out? If so, I could understand. *After all, I felt that way when she and Salvador went for ice cream without me,* I thought, then sat back quickly in the booth. Ethel, Vito's wife and joint owner of the pizza parlor, banged down on the table tall glasses of soda.

"Guess you want one too," she said, and walked off before Anna could answer.

Salvador rummaged through a basket of pencils and crayons that Vito's provided, then began to draw on the paper tablecloth. It was a girl in bell-bottoms and a vest—his retro uniform.

"I've been thinking a lot today," Anna said.

"That's how you get in trouble," Salvador remarked, then drew a boy with pants up to his armpits—the nerdo uniform. "What have you been thinking about?" he went on.

"Everything," she said softly. Their eyes met for a moment, then Anna turned to me. "Is your ecology article going to be in the next edition?"

"No," I told her, "it's in the trash can. *My* trash can."

Her eyes widened. "Why?"

"Because I didn't want to have to wear a bag over my head the day the *Spectator* came out."

Salvador drew a huge pair of glasses, the kind Charlie wore. *The Spectacles,* he wrote in block letters that looked just like the typeface that headed the front page of the *Spectator.*

"I didn't want people to read it," I explained. "That's why I hadn't told you or Salvador that I wrote it. My article stank." I looked her in the eye. "I quit today, Anna."

"We quit," Salvador put in. "You were right all along. Besides," he said to Anna with one of his famous eye twinkles, "it wouldn't have been any fun without you to critique the stinky articles and get annoyed at Charlie."

Anna let out a long breath as Salvador drew a big nose, so that the eyeglasses rested on them.

Beneath that, where the *Spectator's* masthead would have said "News and Views," he wrote, "Something Stinks."

Anna and I burst out laughing. I felt a little sad, though. Gone was my built-in excuse to hang with my friends.

Ethel returned and plunked down Anna's soda. "I guess I should tell Vito extra pepperoni," she grumbled, then headed off. "You kids."

We grinned at each other. Ethel always pretended to be gruff, the same way she pretended she couldn't hear you, but she could eavesdrop from four tables away. Everybody knew she looked out for the kids who came to her pizza parlor.

Salvador began to draw a picture of Ethel. While he sketched, I wrote on the tablecloth:

Miss Perfect's Guide to Manners When Eating at Vito's

(1) The polite eater does not let strings of mozzarella stretch more than four inches between his mouth and the pizza. (2) If it does, the polite eater does not make loud noises and point to the cheese. Also, he does not twirl his tongue like a fishing

reel to suck it in. (3) When sharing a pizza, polite eaters—

"That's it," Anna said suddenly. "That's it!"
Salvador and I looked up. "What's it?" he asked.
She took a thick green crayon and started drawing rectangles around our scribblings. Then she made other boxes, writing in at the top of one "School Menu for This Week" and in another "A Report on the Bored of Education."
I watched her a moment, then said, "It looks like a layout for a newspaper."
Anna cocked an eyebrow. "What do you think?"
"I don't *think*. I *know*," Salvador said, "that they're never going to let us do any of this stuff."
But I saw the brightness in Anna's eyes and suddenly guessed her idea. "Which doesn't mean we can't do it," I said. Of course! That was the answer to everything! "Exactly! We can—with the three of us as editors," Anna replied excitedly. "Think about it. There's got to be a mountain of good stuff we can publish, stories and art by us and by other kids who've given up on the *Spectator*."
"Our own newspaper . . . ," Salvador said, his dark eyes shining.
"How about doing a magazine instead?" I suggested. "That would let us try all kinds of things."

"Good idea!" Anna replied.

"We can print whatever we want," Salvador said.

"Yeah—yeah," Ethel muttered, coming up behind us and shoveling a pizza off a big board. It was crusted over with pepperoni. "Sounds great—you can do whatever you want. But take it from Vito and me—starting up on your own is harder than you think."

The three of us glanced at each other.

"There'll be a lot of work. A lot of squabbling," she warned. "And as for money—hoo, boy! You want something to argue about—try where you get the dough to carry out your big plans."

"We're not opening a restaurant, Ethel," Salvador pointed out.

"Mostly what we need is paper," Anna said.

"Yeah, the green kind, with Tom Jefferson's picture on it," Ethel replied.

I knew she was right. Even if we used home computers, publishing something like a magazine would cost us.

Anna crossed her arms over her chest stubbornly. "I still want to do it."

"Me too," I said. "There must be a way."

"I've got a zillion ideas for cartoons," Salvador added.

"So, what I suggest," Ethel went on, "if you'd just let me get a word in edgewise, is that Vito and I buy some advertising space in your magazine to help with the costs."

My mouth dropped open. "You'd do that?" I asked.

"Really?" Anna echoed.

Ethel pointed to Salvador's drawing of her, her gray eyes glittering. "Of course, you got to put in a better picture of me."

"Madame," Salvador said in his most gallant tone, "that is an excellent bargain."

Jessica

As it turned out, I didn't throw up. More important, when the scores were finally added, SVJH had won the meet.

"The way you pulled together as a team—every one of you—it makes me want to weep like a proud mum," Krebsy told us as we climbed onto the minibus. She stopped me before I got on. "Jessica, you were brilliant today," she said.

Suddenly I felt like third place was pretty okay. In fact, it seemed *better* than okay. "Thanks, Mrs. Krebs," I said.

When we arrived at school, Lana suggested that we celebrate our victory at Vito's. Krebsy had to get home, but she waited while we phoned our parents from the school's athletic office. Twelve of us got permission to go to the pizza shop, and we all decided to wear our uniforms.

"Let's walk in like jocks," Bonnie said. "Let's strut like a football team."

We made a big entrance. Then I discovered my sister there with her friends.

"How'd you do?" Elizabeth asked me, laughing.

I gave her the victory sign. Anna smiled, and El Salvador stood up and applauded. I gave him a bow—for once, I didn't want to strangle him.

My teammates and I pushed several tables together and sat down. Ethel carried over frosty pitchers of water. "You girls ready to order?"

We all spoke at the same time.

"We're ready."

"We're starved—bring anything."

"Could we see a menu?"

"I can't stand artichokes."

"You mean anchovies."

"Either one. Do you have sweet sausage?"

"Who's got money?"

"I have fifty-one cents."

"Everybody dig for money!"

Ethel threw her hands in the air and walked away. We all started digging in our gym bags to see how many dollars we had between us.

"Bethel," I said as I searched my bag, "at the end of the race—um—thanks for pulling me up."

"No problem," she replied. "In math class, thanks for backing me up."

"You mean telling the truth? You're supposed to do that anyway."

She lifted her eyebrows. "Did that make it any easier?" she asked.

"No," I admitted. "I probably lost a friend."

"Lose one, gain one."

I looked up at her. Was Bethel a new friend? I hoped so.

Bethel kept fishing through her gym bag, and I went back to digging for money. When I lifted the towel, there were my disgusting old trainers, still damp from the week before. Ick. I pulled them out and set them down on the paper tablecloth.

"Whew!" Lana said. "They must use really old cheese in this place."

"It's the shoes," Ginger observed.

"Shoes belong on the floor," Ethel told me, swinging by our table to drop a fistful of knives and forks on it with a loud clatter. "And those belong in the trash."

"Yeah, trash 'em," Bethel said. "Those shoes have never run so slow since being on *your* feet, Jessica."

So she *did* know about the shoes all along! I grinned at her, and she grinned back. "Trash 'em?" I replied. "When they brought us good luck? When I paid one whole dollar for Bethel McCoy originals?"

Bethel laughed. "Guess that makes us *sole* mates," she said, tying one trainer to my gym bag, the other one to hers. "Here's double good luck for our next meet, girlfriend!"

156